A JIGSAW of FIRE and STARS

ALSO BY YABA BADOE

A Jigsaw of Fire and Stars

WOLF LIGHT

YABA BADOE

ZEPHYR

An imprint of Head of Zeus

First published in the UK in 2019 by Zephyr,
an imprint of Head of Zeus Ltd

9 7 5 3 1 2 4 6 8

A catalogue record for this book is available from
the British Library.

ISBN (HB): 9781786695512
ISBN (E): 9781786695505

Typeset by Ed Pickford

Printed and bound in Great Britain by
CPI Group (UK) Ltd, Croydon CRO 4YY

Head of Zeus Ltd
First Floor East
5–8 Hardwick Street
London EC1R 4RG

WWW.HEADOFZEUS.COM

For Colin – my One and Only!

'A girl's voice doesn't break:
it gets firmer.'

Ama Ata Aidoo, 'A Young Woman's Voice'

Ice melts
In a trickle, then a stream
Until oceans swell and
Sea salt loses its tang.

Waves surge in a crush of rainfall and flood
Pulverising earth to mud.
Cliffs bloat and crumble
Oozing fossil and flint.
Rivers course over banks.
Trees and houses tumble
Roofs fly in the sky.

Stitch by stitch
As the earth's tapestry unravels
Monsters rip through snag and snarl.
Sky-swallowers, soil-eaters, blood-suckers:
Skin-walkers all.

Are you ready to ride the whirlwind?

* * *

I

Zula

*

My name is Zula, the name my father gave me an hour before I was born. On that day as I journeyed into the world, Pa saw the light of the evening star in the sky. The planet Venus was turning to play with Jupiter, and struck by her brilliance, Pa stood and stared. He's a healer, a shaman with an intuition so mighty, he navigates pathways between this realm and another glazed with stardust and spirit.

Entranced, goose-bumps pimpling his arms, Pa decided I would be called Zula. Along with my name came an awakening confirmed by Venus' smile that night. From the beginning, Pa believed that my sisters and I were destined to shape the world. I would be one of three, a pride of sisters. Born in different hemispheres – in forest, desert and by water – together, we would dance with creation and replenish it.

The first time he told me the story of my birth, Pa described the scene as if he could still see it. The sun, setting over snow-capped peaks, burned the Altai Mountains gold. The foothills beneath glowed; so much so, that a flat stretch of scrubland in front of it shone.

'Even the air seemed to sparkle,' Pa said. 'Without a horse's breath of wind, the world stood still and glimmered like kindling: grasses, bushes, trees, all of it, from the faraway mountains to our homestead.'

'That summer, we were camped beside a lake, Zula. At the water's edge our horses and camels were grazing. In wolf-light, water that flickers blue in the day, takes on a haunted, purple hue. Dogs feel the heat of fangs in their teeth and cows, butting like bulls, recall the maul of horns on their heads. That's when you burst into our lives, my daughter.'

I was born after the big winter thaw, at the start of the grazing season. Mongolia, my home is a land of mountains, lakes and sky – an ocean of sky. We're nomads, often on the move, in search of pasture for our animals. It was into this world that I emerged blue-eyed, a silver curl on my head.

After I took my first breath, Pa claimed that instead of crying, I sang a desert song – a piercing note that I held for so long that my grandmother, fearing I was a spirit child and my first breath would be my last, slapped me.

'You know your grandmother,' Pa said.

I nodded. Grandma, Pa's mother, the leader of Pa's circle, is not the easiest of women to be around. At times her tongue can be as sharp as the bite of a sabre-toothed tiger and yet she guides me nonetheless.

Within six weeks, though the coil on my head remained silver, the colour of my eyes shifted from blue to grey – pale grey like the fur of a wolf in winter. 'My winter wolf,' Grandma called me. More convinced than ever that my time on earth would be precious, she swaddled me and kept me close, while Ma went back to her chores.

Grandma petted me, fed me bone broth to build me up and anchor me to Mother Earth. She rubbed herbs on my scalp to encourage my hair to grow. She smeared ointments and lotions, whispered magic words on my crown. And when, at last, my hair emerged, it dazzled like lightning in snow.

As I grew older, capable of placing one foot in front of the other, Grandma taught me language and told me tales of the Great Khan who forged our nation and launched the Mongol Empire. Tales of the mighty swords he wielded: scimitars, sabres, Mongolian ilds; swords as powerful as Grandma's spirit. To bind me to her craft, she held me transfixed with fables of night and day creatures that dwell on the steppes. Then, a twinkle in her eyes, she spoke of their companions, women warriors, archers on horseback, nomads like us.

Between them, Grandma and Pa saw the framework of a picture my mother was unable to see. They saw and heard. And what they understood, they passed on to me. Of the three of us sisters, I, the firstborn, was the leader. The heartwood that would bind us was that each of us would have a teacher and mentor to help us excel in our craft, and each of us a special place to take care of.

In my case, we were on our annual journey from our summer grazing grounds to the outskirts of the town where we winter when I saw mine – a range of mountains shaped like a giant in hibernation. I froze, for there he was stretched on the horizon, his body carved in the peaks and craters ahead of us.

'Pa, can you see what I see?' I asked.

Aged seven, I was on horseback with my father. Perched in front, I sheltered in his arms.

'What do you see, my daughter?'

'There's a giant fast asleep in those rocks over there.' I pointed. 'There's his head and his arms. One day I'm going to wake him up, Pa!'

My father laughed. 'Clever girl! I didn't register him until I was twice your age. I couldn't see the giant even when your grandmother told me to look out for it. My brother, Batu, saw him first.'

'How could you not see him, Pa?' With a finger I traced the turban on the giant's head, and on his feet boots a thousand times bigger than those worn by the Great Khan. 'You see now, don't you?'

Pa reined in his horse, a white stallion he called Takhi. 'Indeed, I do,' he replied.

He dropped me to the ground, jumped down, and taking my hand, said as we strolled towards the mountains: 'Now that you've seen him, Zula, if I were to ask you, would you be willing to watch over him?'

I gazed at my father's face, a face flushed by wind and sun.

'Well, Zula?'

I hesitated, looked at the sleeping giant and then back at my father. His head, covered in a fur hat, tilted as his eyes posed the question a second time.

I am a shaman's daughter, attuned to the spinning of cobwebs and the secrets of murmuring hearts. I am my father's treasure, even though Grandma's constant refrain is: 'Tread carefully on the course we've set you on, Zula! A shaman's journey is dangerous. Some of us lose our way in the realm of spirits and fail to find a place in this one, like my son Batu. He fled to the city instead.'

I shushed Grandma's whisper. This wasn't like being told to look after my brothers, or milk our animals and gut fish with my mother. This was special.

I looked, nodded and felt the stirring of an emotion I was able to taste but didn't understand. Drops of honey laced with horse's milk drizzled in my mouth. My heart tingled.

'It'll take commitment,' said Pa.

'Will it be for ever?'

'Would you like that?'

'Yes,' I replied. 'The big man up there needs someone to look after him, same as you do, Pa.'

'Well said, my daughter. But are you willing to spend hours alone with him to assure him he's remembered? Are you prepared to be an apprentice and learn our craft?'

I nodded a second time.

'Very well,' said Pa, 'from now until your services are no longer needed, you will be the guardian of the Sleeping Giant of the Mountains.'

The following spring, on our way to our summer grazing grounds, the rest of the family went on ahead while Pa took me for a closer inspection of the colossus in the rocks.

After the long freeze of winter, snow was melting, making the terrain slippery. Tufts of scrub sprouted around boulders, and yet up we climbed, deep into the mountains until we turned towards a crater, which from a distance formed the Giant's mouth. Clumps of wildwood brushed against us, but as the gaping fracture loomed above, any hint of trees was left behind.

We rode in silence; the only sound the thud of Takhi's hooves as he picked his way. The further we rode, the more I bristled as pinpricks of tension settled around my neck. The air stirred. I heard a swoosh of wings, a scuffle, the frantic bleating of a mountain goat, a yelp.

Nostrils flaring, Takhi whinnied. I stroked his mane to reassure him, and in so doing, comforted myself. 'There's no need to be frightened,' I murmured, 'there's no need to worry. We're safe 'cause we're with Pa.'

I tried to remain calm even as I imagined Ma shaking her head as she bellowed: 'Husband, what are you doing? Our daughter is eight years old! She knows her left from her right, but she is still a child, I tell you! A child!'

I trembled as every once in a while I touched Pa's hand to remind myself that I was not alone. The higher we climbed, the more desolate and harsh the landscape, the more lonely I became. If it hadn't been for the warmth of Takhi beneath us, I could have believed that Pa and I were the only creatures alive. I shivered.

'Is the mountain speaking to you, Zula, my girl?'

'Is this how it talks?' I replied. 'By making me feel small? Smaller even than the tiniest of Ma's needles!'

Pa laughed, a laugh that echoing over ravines ricocheted back. 'These mountains speak by demanding our respect. They were here long before the first of our ancestors was born.'

'Even before the Great Khan?'

'Even before him, Zula. We're entering star time now, where to be human is to gaze at the heavens and understand that we too are made of stardust. Star time is where we seek wisdom, discover our true purpose and live in awe of this.' Pa waved his hand in a gesture that encircled every crag and cranny. The circle complete, his fingers touched his chest where his heart lay beating.

'In awe,' I repeated. So that was what I was feeling: as wary as a wagtail, an eagle towering above it. And yet behind my twitchiness were new emotions that tipped me into wonder, feeding a hunger I didn't know I had.

A few kilometres later, the ground beneath us changed again. There was no earth to speak of, simply smatterings of soil that yielded sprigs of needle grass. We trekked upwards, ever upwards, along a trail that led through a pass on to a ledge. There we dismounted.

Pa removed a saddlebag from his horse, belted it around his waist, and tied Takhi to a wooden spike. I wondered if perhaps Grandma had brought Pa to this place.

'We'll be back in the morning, old boy,' Pa said, stroking Takhi's forehead. The horse settled in the shelter of a rock while Pa and I clambered up the trail.

The sun's rays were beginning to fade and a north wind moaned, chilling my hands and feet.

'We're almost there, Zula,' said Pa sensing my unease.

He lifted me onto a ridge and heaved himself up

beside me, a steep canyon on one side, a glowering granite promontory on the other.

Condensation made the surface of these rocks even more perilous than those below. I slipped and would have tumbled, if Pa hadn't grabbed my hand and steadied me.

'Careful,' he said. 'Not much further now.'

We staggered on, inching our way forwards.

What looked like the Giant's mouth from a distance was, in fact, a rocky indentation, a nesting ground for eagles. At the sound of our footfall, our slip and slide on slabs, eagles took to the air and circled. Heart hammering, I counted seven of them. One flew close, so close that as it banked, I gasped at the size of its talons.

'They think we're going to steal their eaglets,' Pa explained. 'They're trying to distract us. This way, Zula.'

We walked carefully along a ridge, then down a sweep of fir trees. Pa directed me beyond them, to the entrance of a cave overlooking the Giant's mouth.

It was late afternoon by now, about half an hour before dusk. The sun, gliding behind the mountain, dappled the valley gold. Shafts of light illuminated the sky, streaking it turquoise above, while elsewhere it glowed indigo blue.

On this, my first expedition alone with my father, my empty stomach growled reminding me of home.

Ma would be cooking by now. If I was with her, I would soon be fed and warm. Instead, I was perched at the entrance of a cave, the wind stinging my cheeks as my fingers froze.

From the pouch at his waist, Pa removed his small shaman's drum. Then to my surprise, he covered my shoulders with a shawl and handed me a wedge of dried sheep's meat.

'Eat what you can,' he said. 'It'll keep you warm.'

Ravenous, I began to chew while Pa started tapping his drum and murmuring. I've seen my father enter the realm of spirits many times. That's what a shaman does: speaks to beings others can't see to maintain a balance between us humans, Mother Earth and Father Sky. Balance and harmony, Pa says, give us good health and food to eat.

In as much as a child was able to, I understood what my father did. This time, I reckoned, was going to be no different. Or so I thought, until Pa took out his special shaman's smock, which he wears at New Year festivals and pulled it on. A swathe of heavy silk cotton, white in colour, encrusted with silver mirrors to reflect the beauty of our surroundings, it shimmered and flowed as Pa began to dance.

I savoured the taste of meat on my tongue. My blood quickened and as warmth trickled through my fingers once again, I trembled, listening. A moment later I heard it: tingling tension accompanied by a faint hum that resonated from Pa's drum. Pa may have been beating the same old rhythm and swaying to his usual song, but this time the effect was electric.

Wind tunnelled through the fir trees below and with its hiss came the sharp-pitched snarl of a wildcat, the bark of a solitary wolf, the faint snuffling of bear cubs. The pulse of my father's drum, mingled with the flapping of eagle wings, vibrated in my ears. My heart began to race as a curious sensation convulsed my body, reminding me of times when I turned round and the world spun about me.

The earth rippled, and in that instant, my father appeared to merge into the landscape. I did as well. I soared with him as he transported us to a secret place that existed in front of our eyes.

In wolf-light my skin sparkled. And when I gazed at my father amazed, I was struck by the reflection of my eyes in his, and how the grey in them and the silver curl on my forehead glittered diamond bright.

Weightless, I danced with my father, twisting and turning to the beat of his drum, whirling around the mirrors of his shaman's smock. I danced, and between one step and the next, others appeared alongside us: my sisters and their teachers.

My heart leaped, for I felt I'd always known them. Adoma, an Ashanti: dark-eyed, skin the purple-black of a juniper berry, hair cropped short, tinged russet-red like an apple. In her shadow, I glimpsed a faint feline form, lithe and poised, and looming above her the lanky frame of her grandfather.

Linet, hair the colour of night, tawny of eye, rosy-cheeked; a Celt from Cornwall. On her shoulder, a glint of a black-feathered bird, red-beaked with matching red feet. Behind her, an old woman with a shiny, round face. In a blink of an eye, my grandmother appeared.

It was then I felt a creature curl around my ankle nibbling my toes. I saw a flicker of white – a wolf cub's tail. One moment it was there, then the cub vanished. And of our teachers, only Pa remained.

Yet somehow, though I couldn't quite see them, those shadowy creatures that adorned us existed as our pride of three stared at each other, revelling in the mystery we were a part of. We stared, then guided by instinct formed a circle around Pa.

As soon as our fingers touched, we remembered. Fragments, then smouldering tales of the past flamed. Memories, long suppressed, flowed through our veins reminding us of vows taken before we were born and all that had happened since we drew breath. Our thoughts flew from one to the other replaying our early steps, our favourite games, sharing the faces of those we loved best. We untangled knotted secrets, until Pa, having sung a song to creation from the back of his throat, gave us our mission.

'We live in dangerous times,' he said, 'when the

balance between our worlds has broken. Mother Earth is on fire, Father Sky weeps tears of blood. We live at a time when money is more powerful than human life and skin-walkers stalk the earth trampling all in their path: trees, rivers, mountains, forests – even the mightiest of oceans and everything within them – are their prey these days. But with our craft, my daughters, we can defeat those who live for money alone without thought of the future; those who destroy whatever they touch because they live without heart.'

Eyes ablaze, Pa fixed his gaze on us. 'This is what I ask of you: that you outwit and sabotage skin-walkers everywhere to protect our sacred sites from their scourge.'

In a heartbeat my sisters and I agreed.

'Very good,' Pa replied: 'Now you must choose a word; a word with the power to transport you into star time the moment you say it.'

Adoma turned to me; Linet did too as I recalled a sound, the cry of a huntress to her eagle.

'Let us use the hunter's call,' I suggested. 'At any hint of danger, or if we want to talk, we'll use it as a signal.'

Pa nodded.

'*Hukaa*!' I hollered. '*Hukaa*!' My voice rang over the Giant's mouth, and my sisters echoed me.

At last, when dark fingers of night had all but

smothered wolf-light, Pa pressed his thumb on the inside of my wrist. Pain darted down my fingers. I flexed them. The throbbing eased and while Pa did the same to my sisters, I examined the patch of skin over my pulse. Bit by bit a tattoo of an eight-pronged star set in deepest blue emerged: a star with a hole in the middle.

Adoma looked at an identical mark on her wrist. 'My grandfather's shown me this sign before,' she said. 'It's *adinkra*, from Ghana.'

'Yes,' Pa replied. '*Nsoromma*, a symbol of guardianship. You three are now children of the sky and guardians of the earth. Connected by stardust, you will hear the earth's call and become attuned to her pain and joy. All you have to do is say the word you've chosen when you touch your tattoo, and you'll be able to talk to each other in star time and in shadow. Better still, align yourselves with *nsoromma* and your gifts will grow.'

Moonlight flickered on our faces. We murmured, '*Nsoromma*,' and a word new to my tongue settled on it with the ease of an old friend.

I touched Pa's hand. His smile gathered me in.

'Zula, my daughter,' he said. 'I named you for your radiance. In time your gift of sight will help you dazzle our foes with a blink of your eyes.'

I rubbed the star and sensed the shine in me deepen as the world about me glowed.

'You, Adoma,' Pa continued, 'are named for your grace and strength of spirit. As your spirit grows so too will your mastery of what is unseen to the human eye. Should skin-walkers venture within seven paces of you, use what is hidden to assail them.'

'And you, Little Linet,' said Pa to my sister who was not little at all, but a full head taller than Adoma and I. 'You are a truth-teller named after your element, water. Your gift, mocked in your country as a scold's tongue, is one that probes to uncover what is hidden. Before long you'll see that the lake of tears within you, the lake that moistens your tongue and fingertips, is a blessing to Mother Earth.'

Pa closed his eyes, and smoothing his right hand over our wrists said, 'Unless you choose otherwise, these tattoos bind you, and by entwining your thoughts make them as clear as water to each of you. No one else can see them but members of our craft.'

'We don't have much time,' he added. 'From what I've glimpsed, the odds are against us. Learn what you have to quickly and be brave, for your teachers and I won't always be with you.'

Pa paused.

'May you pursue a righteous path.
May the earth always nourish you.
May your gifts grow with your years.
May no skin-walker escape your grasp.

And may nsoromma keep you safe
As you sing your heart's song.'

Pa tapped our wrists with his shaman's drum. One tap, two; on the third, my sisters disappeared.

Linet

※ ※

Next morning we begin learning the craft. Nana's been teaching me since my thumb was as small as the toe of a frog, but after meeting my sisters and becoming one of three, a star on my wrist, I *crave* the craft.

'That's sister-magic,' Nana Merrimore says. 'Those girls are filling a hole in your heart. Must be, because now not only are you swimming in water, you're jumping when you hit the ground as well.'

That's Nana for you. Talks in picture-book language. Baby talk. Talks too much, sometimes, if you ask me. Not that you'd have asked my opinion back then. I was still a child, see.

I'm Linet, the middle sister of three, Nana Merrimore's water baby, the granddaughter she caught as I slid into the world. Nana's fingers were the first I clasped in my birthing pool. And when my mother abandoned me soon after, Nana raised me and made me her own.

The lake I'm named after, a drowning pool for witches in days gone by, looms into view from my window. The first thing I see when I wake and the last before I sleep is the lake I care for.

We start by having our lessons in star time, by the Linet Lake, far from prying eyes. Star time's everywhere if you know how to find it. Nana says that once you do, it's easy as pie to step in and out of. It's all about breath, see. About finding a calm space within that allows your spirit to slip through a crease in time to the heart of creation.

Before dinosaurs, before we crawled out of the sea, there was star time. If you can't find a crinkle to sneak through, often nature takes you there. Hold her hand, climb a mountain. Walk by the sea, by the river where Adoma's shrine is. In forest, woodland, desert or moor, star time rolls you between her palms until you're winnowed clean.

Nana introduces our first lesson half-singing, swaying:

'Soft now and listen.
 Hear what I say
 And let it stay.'

She pauses. Eyes fastened on her, our minds hooked,
she chants, hauling us in:

'*Magic comes naturally*
Sight, sound, taste and touch,
It's in our senses.
Earth, sky, wind, fire
And water.

There are no secrets to uncover in our craft,
No spells to cast.
Once you know who you are
Magic flows.

Learn to listen and be still.
Put your ear on a tree
Hear it grow.

See that adder on a rock?
Imagine you're its shadow,
And as your minds lock
Feel the sun on your skin
Let it tow you in.

Touch, tease, learn to freeze
Above all breathe
Hear creatures great and small
Whisper in song and story
Hearts beat in magic glory.'

Zula, Adoma and I, hungry as chicks in the nest, swallow Nana's rhyme whole. My sisters' hands brush against mine and I chuckle, murmuring: 'Easy peasy.'

'Koko!' Adoma whispers. Easy as corn-meal porridge!

Between the three of us, we believe we already understand what Nana's saying. Nonetheless, she repeats the rhyme encouraging us to recite it with her as she points to her senses and the elements we work with: earth, sky, fire and water. The more we say the words, the more we're convinced they were engrained in us long ago. So, without any prompting, I take my sisters to a grove of oak trees by the Linet Lake. In real time the trees are hobbled, blasted by wind and age. Today, they're young and sturdy, branches stretching to touch the sun.

We press our ears to a trunk. We focus; hear the rise and trickle of sap. Bark crackles and creaks. Roots creep and tickle as they suck and seek. The tree sighs. Leaves rustle and bit-by-bit, those sheltering within reveal themselves. First a blackbird, then an exaltation of skylarks sing, splashing us with song until the blackbird, piqued by our interest, swoops.

We settle in its shadow. Head cocked, the bird hops closer. Eyes gleaming, it pecks at smatterings of moss that grow by the lake. Its orange beak digs and neck flung back, the bird swallows a grub.

It's then, when our minds lock, that I feel it. My

sisters do too, because the three of us gasp as a quiver of bird-life flits through us.

The blade of orange strikes again. Before it jabs a third time it's not only the bird, that blazing inside us, but the moss, the lake, purple-blue irises at the lake's edge. Beyond, on a gentle slope of moor, fern and heather, even patches of stubble grass sing so loudly, we can't help but hear.

Zula smiles: 'Music,' she says. 'All around is music!'

Nose scrunched in surprise, Adoma asks: 'Have you heard the grass sing before?'

Zula nods and we inch closer.

Zula fingers the midnight brightness of my hair. I smooth a palm over her silver hair, while with the other I stroke Adoma's russet crown. Our heads tilt, our foreheads touch, and as Zula's curl tickles my brow, a forgotten memory unpeels.

I'm a toddler sitting on the floor of Nana's kitchen. Mrs Gribble, Nana's helper, is washing pans in the sink. Her two sons are with us: Lance and Arthur. Arthur, older than me, runs round the kitchen while Lance, as uncertain on his feet as I am, waddles close by.

When I stick my tongue out at him, Lance totters towards me, and following my lead we touch tongues. Arthur, not to be left out, joins in our feast of slurps and licks before Mrs Gribble turns.

'Stop that,' she hisses. 'That girl's a Merrimore and they're trouble, I tell you! Trouble!'

Language is beyond me, but the ferocity in Mrs Gribble's hiss burns and I flinch as the toddler I once was cries.

'Is there a problem out there?' Nana's voice drifts in from next door.

'We're fine,' says Mrs Gribble. She pulls us apart and scooping me up from the floor, pats my back.

I'm like a hen trapped in a coop, a fox on the prowl, whenever Mrs Gribble's around. Even so, in star time, the taste of her boys' tongues lingers on mine; a taste of blackberries dipped in cream: luscious.

Tongue drenched, another memory clutches my throat. I shake my head, try to push it away, but like a leaping frog, it slips through and I gag. Above me are ripples of water through which I see my mother's face as her tears splash the Linet Lake. Her tears flow through me and I sob.

'Linet, are you all right? Girls!'

Trembling, I tell Nana I'm fine. 'Zula, how do you do it?' I whisper.

Zula places a palm on my brow and the hurt disappears.

'How?' Adoma echoes, for she saw the Gribbles too and felt the throb of my mother's heartache.

'I'm a shaman's daughter,' Zula replies.

'And I'm a Merrimore! We're water witches, we are! We're born in water and return to it when we die!' My eyes narrow as grey ones burrow into mine.

Zula blinks, then explains: 'In the same way that the grass sings, so do we. Everything's connected, especially us three.'

'So?' I say.

'Don't you want to hear your heart's song?' she asks.

Adoma nods. I do too, even though neither of us is sure what Zula means.

'If you want to sing your song fully,' she goes on, 'you have to know yourself and remember good as well as bad things that have happened to you.'

'I don't want to remember *everything*,' I reply. 'Not the bad bits at any rate.'

Adoma shrugs. 'I know the bad already. Ask me and I'll tell you plain-plain: my mother and her okra mouth!'

Zula laughs.

I giggle, a peal that flips into a squeal of terror. 'What if the bad things are so bad, it's best not to know?'

'Then your gift won't grow,' Zula claims.

'Oh, but it will. With us beside you it will,' says Adoma. She takes my hand and strokes it, caressing my fingers. 'If it wasn't for my gran-pa and my one, true friend, Kofi, I wouldn't be as you see me here. Gran-pa-love and Kofi-love make me happy.'

Adoma grins: a grin so mighty, I can't help but confide.

'My mother left me before I had memories to

remember her by. All I have of her are Nana's photographs, yet Nana won't talk about her.'

Adoma lifts my hand and rubbing it against her cheek, folds it in hers. She smiles, a smile that steals into me covering the hole in my heart. My lips twitch and before I know it, I'm smiling as well.

❦

'Linet, my child, you should do everything with intent. What's your intent now, this very moment?'

Three years have passed and Adoma's grandfather – Okomfo Gran-pa – is teaching us the rudiments of fire magic. We're at the shrine he looks after with Adoma. Beside a river, in the middle of a forest near their home, the glade of hardwood trees, graced with mangos and guavas, winks in wolf-light. Even in star time, dusk comes quickly here. It says 'hallo', then leaves with a hasty 'goodbye' within half an hour. Yet as soon as it arrives at the end of a humid day, it throws a golden sheen over orchids, pineapples and palms, soothing the ache behind eyes as tired as mine.

'Linet, did you hear me?'

'I did Gran-pa. It's just that...' I flex my fingers, flick them, and then palm open, raise my hand. Nothing happens.

'Try again, child.'

Once again, nothing. I'm gnarled and knotted, an ignoramus, a waste of space not even I would talk to.

A bead of sweat dribbles down the side of my face. Fingers moisten, become clammy. Why can't I do what I'm supposed to with a simple flick of my wrist as my sisters have done?

'Relax, Little Linet,' Gran-pa says.

'How can I relax when I can't do it?'

'Yes you can!' Adoma replies. 'Chill, my sister! Chill, big-time!'

In the boughs of a mahogany tree opposite, a pair of laughing doves cackles.

Tears prick my eyes. I clench my jaw and through gritted teeth, snap: 'How am I supposed to chill when I'm sweating so much, even the birds are laughing at me!'

Adoma chuckles, while Zula says: 'Steady yourself, Linet. Now, think of everything we've learned so far. Remember how quickly you mastered sky magic?'

Gran-pa smiles, nodding in approval as I recall how Zula's pa and grandma took us step by step through the rigours of sky magic: how we learned to rustle wind through the tips of our fingers; how we galvanised clouds and soothed storms by tending our sacred places.

'Everything you do for Mother Earth and Father Sky,' said Grandma, 'everything, no matter how small, helps balance the world and maintain the flow of energy between this realm and another glazed with spirit.' Wrinkled brown as a walnut, Grandma grinned, revealing gaps in her teeth, mischief in cloudy eyes. 'And when I say "you" that includes *you*, Little Linet.'

'Remember how you excelled in water magic, animal and herb-lore,' Zula continues.

I nod.

I remember the squelch of mud between our toes as we followed Nana Merrimore into the Linet Lake: 'Water has memory,' she told us. 'You may not know it yet, girls, but in the same way that every bit of you needs and relishes water, so water remembers you.'

My sisters thrilled at the Linet Lake's kiss. I did too. But before I surrendered to it, I felt the sting of my mother's tears and shuddered.

We dangled our fingers in the lake, fondled the tug of its current as it drew us to a whirl of water at its centre – the drowning pool.

'You must promise never to go anywhere near it,' Nana warned us.

We promised.

'You remember?' asks Zula.

'I do,' I reply.

'Now, think of something, anything, you'd like to set alight,' she says.

'And while you're at it,' Gran-pa adds, 'direct your fingers to the earth. Sense the heat at its centre and let it flow through your palm!'

I do what they tell me, but again not even a puff of smoke or a spark appears.

I try once more, only this time I imagine Mrs Gribble's face and hear the scorching rage in her voice from way back when. Merrimore girls are trouble are we? Well, here's trouble and it's coming right at you, hag!

Every cell in my body flares. Heat surges through my fingers as a tongue of fire darts from my palm. The forest floor flickers and flames, lighting creepers that clamber up the mahogany tree. A flock of doves soars from its branches. The tree shrieks. I scream. A teardrop salts my eye and as it falls, from the same palm from which fire flamed, a torrent of water gushes, quenching everything in its path.

My sisters beam.

'Excellent,' Gran-pa says, clapping his hands.

And for a moment, as my sisters clap as well, I believe that whatever they can do, I can do too.

There are three of us living by the Linet Lake: Nana, her black cat, Bracken, and me. But then again there are others, for Carbilly has been the home of Merrimore women for generations and in the same way that the moor's alive, so too is the cottage.

In the shadows, the house is home to my sisters as

well. Yet the closer we become, the more I realise how different we are.

Take Zula: magic drifts through her like a never-ending dream. As the years pass and her gift deepens, Adoma and I learn as much from her as we do our teachers.

Adoma, as Zula's pa foretold, reveals a talent as she grows for harnessing the nuts and bolts of unseen elements to hurt those who would harm our spaces. I've watched her blast the stump of a tree in anger, smashing it into smithereens. If she'd had a chance to tackle the tree rustlers who cut the tree down, she'd have scorched them as well.

As soon as I've mastered the basics of earth and fire magic, it's as clear as the ripples on the Linet Lake that anger at Mrs Gribble can only get me so far. Rage has its limits, especially when it stains the tongue with the taste of blackberries. The angrier I become, the stronger the tang, the deeper I hunger for what I don't have: magic to stream through me as easily as it does my sisters. My craving swells until a day comes when I begin to dwell on what's holding me back.

We're in wolf-light at the cave of Zula's mountain, which she visits every month at around the same time as Adoma does the river goddess' shrine. My task is to tend to the Linet Lake daily.

The air is chilly at the cave. Even in summer it's winter cold. Blades of sunlight shiver between night and day. Zula, fur-clad, croons a lullaby to her sleeping giant while below a wolf howls, joining in Zula's song. A cloud, brightened by a sickle moon, glimmers in moon-dance.

The wolf bays louder, as one after the other, her pack dotted around the Giant's mouth takes up her serenade. No one can hear me, but as my craving surges, inside I begin to howl too.

Once the Giant is soothed into the deepest depths of slumber, Zula's luminous eyes skim mine searing me with their wolfish shine. She lowers her eyelids, replying to my question before I ask it.

'To release your heart's song, Linet, to become a sky-warrior, a guardian of the earth, your lake must be as the Sleeping Giant is to me – a mother, a father, your best friend.'

'But my mother's tears haunt me, Zula. What's more, Nana Merrimore talks about everything but Mother. Nana won't mention her, won't tell me who my father is.'

'Chill, my sister,' says Adoma. In wolf-light, her features and limbs glint. 'My father doesn't care a pesewa about me. He won't give me a penny. Sometimes it's best to let parents be.'

'I want to know.'

'You didn't before,' Adoma reminds me.

'Zula, can't you dredge up more of my memories?'

'Follow your tongue,' she replies.

'And how's that going to help me?'

Zula licks her lips, then says: 'That taste!'

Straight away, I know what to do.

On the first day of autumn, I set off from Carbilly, past the Linet Lake, across the moor. I walk through brambles and the last of the briar roses to sweeten my mouth.

Bracken, Nana Merrimore's cat, stalks me, trailing my footsteps before padding alongside. Bracken, so called because her green eyes tinged orange, resemble rusty-tipped ferns moist with dew. The only cat I know capable of strolling with a human without being distracted treads daintily. A sedge warbler flits over a willow shrub; Bracken ignores it. A skylark hurls its song at us; the cat seems deaf, then blind to a rabbit that bounds past.

Where I step, Bracken follows. And when I create a veil of drizzle-mist and unfurl it, wrapping it around me to hide behind, Bracken, tail up, moves closer, until back hunched, she pads between my legs almost tripping me. She purrs, her eyes tracking mine as through a haze of vapour they settle on Crow's Nest, home of the Gribbles.

A stone's throw away I hear Mrs Gribble humming as she cooks at a stove.

'Lance! Arthur! Breakfast's ready.'

'Coming, Ma,' the eldest boy replies, while Lance, upstairs, pauses at a window. Puzzled, he stares at the swell and sway of mist outside.

'Lance! Where are you?'

About to turn, he stops. I sniff his scent; inhale a whiff of summer pudding.

Bracken hisses. My fingers flutter, muffling her clamour with another layer of fog. Thickening, it swirls, concealing us. Or so I believe, until the boy at the window sticks out his tongue and laughs.

His warmth licks my skin like a pup, its tail wagging. I bask in his smile, in the gleam of his raven hair. And as the taste of blackberries overwhelms me, I grasp that not only do I want him; I need him to like me best of all.

'*Hukaa*!' Adoma calls from afar. 'Sisters, come quickly!'

I return his smile and flee.

3

Adoma

✳ ✳ ✳

Last but not least, it's *me* – the third-born of three – Adoma. Me, a Ghana-girl through and through, a 100-per-cent-all-the-way Asante Kotoko football supporter. It's my turn to talk now, so listen well, my friend!

The day I summoned my sisters to my sanctuary in star time, Zula arrived first at the river goddess' shrine – the one in the forest.

I'd gone there to practise a dance in praise of the deity who protects our village, our trees and the river; a dance for harvest to thank her for our crops: cassava, cocoa, plantain and yam. My hands and feet were moving to the rhythm of my heart, when the sky cracked open, and in they swarmed: fruit bats – legions of them. Sky foxes on the rampage. *Chomp! Chomp!*

I tried to shoo them away, but within seconds, all I could do was watch as tiny teeth savaged the fruit of the guava trees. Guavas ravaged! Every pineapple devoured! Every mango, I tell you! *Aba*! Come and see!

I would have blasted them back into the sky had it not been for the vows we live by, my sisters and I. We've sworn never to harm the creatures that seek refuge in our sacred places. The only sacrifices we make are gifts of the heart in which no blood is spilled, no life taken – unless we meet skin-walkers intent on destruction.

That day, Okomfo Gran-pa was out of town in Accra visiting my mother. I was alone, so I rubbed the tattoo on my wrist and summoned my sisters with the huntress' call.

As soon as she arrived, Zula surveyed the scene: a camp of bats dangling from trees shorn of fruit. Trees Gran-pa had planted to mark the boundaries of our shrine. Zula's face confirmed what I already knew. This was bad, so bad, it was unlike anything we'd experienced.

'This shouldn't be happening,' she said. 'Not here.'

'Well, it's happened. If what's going on in the real world is beginning to affect us here, it's going to get much worse over there.'

Zula nodded.

A moment later, Linet surfaced. Flushed, she gaped

horrified at the dark, bulbous fruit quivering on trees: winged foxes at rest.

Panic hastened my breath as Zula spoke: 'This breach is a sign, an omen that something bad is about to happen in real time. I feel it.'

'Me too,' said Linet with a shiver.

Fear shimmied down my spine. We'd been training for this moment most of our lives, but as I heard trouble slither towards us, it held me, transfixed.

Linet rubbed the goose-bumps prickling her arms. 'You can't hear when a tree is cut down on the other side of the world, but before long we're living with the fallout.'

'Only next time, it will be worse,' I said. 'A plague of locusts or that red tide rising along the coast of Florida.'

My sisters' eyes probed mine, questioning, so I described what I'd seen on television: a deadly red algae ravishing the straits the other side of the Atlantic, killing fish, turtles and dolphins while the stench of rotting corpses fouled beaches.

'*Mother Earth is on fire, Father Sky weeps tears of blood*,' I murmured, repeating the words of Zula's father.

I straightened my back, made a fist of my hand: 'There will soon be skin-walkers here…'

'Not if we can help it,' said Linet. 'But what do we do about these bats?'

'They might as well stay,' Zula replied. 'They've

eaten all the fruit. Before long they too will be food for wild cats and owls.'

'First,' I said, 'we should conceal the crack in the sky to prevent any more intruders. Then we get ready for what lies ahead. Let's do it, my sisters!'

So we did. With a combination of water and sky magic we covered the breach with clouds. Linet created mist with her fingers, which Zula compacted into rolling puffs of cumulus. Then, using the power of my mind and the energy around us, I flung them up, arranging them to disguise the chasm and prevent it from widening.

Each of us knew this was a temporary measure; a gesture as futile as sticking a finger in a dyke to prevent a raging flood. All the same, we thought it best we did what we could.

'I'll tell Grandma and Pa what's happening here,' said Zula before she vanished.

Heart heavy, no longer in the mood to dance, I sat by the river, Linet beside me. She slipped her hand over mine and as her touch settled, I sensed a change in her, a sizzle that hadn't been present before.

'Eh-eh, have you followed your tongue already?'

'Yes,' she smiled, her head falling on my shoulder.

'My sister, don't play with me. Tell me! What happened?'

'A glut of blackberries,' she sighed. 'My tongue's fizzing, my skin's ablaze with Lance's smile.'

'And?'

'He sees me, Adoma. No one else does when I roam the moor wrapped in drizzle-mist. Only him.'

'Maybe he's special.'

A family of otters slipped into the river: a mother and her pups. Their skill in water, the deftness of their claws, bodies and teeth as they fished, never ceased to amaze me.

'You think he's special, do you?'

'What does your heart tell you, Linet?'

'If my tongue's connected to my heart, maybe he is.'

I chuckled. 'Then do what you have to, my sister. Come! Let's swim.'

We tore off our clothes and hand in hand jumped.

As the river gurgled above me, a thought swam in my mind: after what had happened here today perhaps this was my last dip with otters at the goddess' shrine.

Surfacing for air, I whispered:

'Goddess of forest and river,
Protector of life, I call on you.
Breath, blood, tree and stone,
Deliver us from skin-walkers!
Fish, bud, bee and bone.
May those who stalk us fester,
As soon as they enter your sanctuary.'

The leaves of a mahogany tree rustled on branches that dipped and swayed. A sign, I believed, that having heard me, the river goddess would answer my prayer.

4

I am wolf.

Snuffling and tumbling, I romp, alive to the smile of the moon as she turns her back on the sun. The crescent fades, the globe blooms and I yelp. Wriggling and rolling, tail curled, I sniff and snort. A plume of steam swirls from my nostrils and I sneeze as wind shrieks over the Giant's mouth.

A she-wolf growls, assembling a pack of sisters to hunt.

'Wait for me!' I try to tell them. But no matter how hard I strive, I can't shape words on my tongue. Instead, I whine, excited at the scent of deer drifting from below. I want to run with the pack, but with the wobbly legs of a whelp, I don't have the strength to bound and tack, as I should.

I grizzle, warm my nose with a flick of my tail. Raise my head to howl, but the sound I make, the yap-snap of a pup, sets the she-wolves baying.

I wait in the warmth of the den, sniffing for clues as to what lies ahead.

I am wolf.

And one day soon, I shall hunt with my pack.

5
Linet

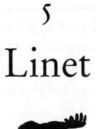

There are rules to using our craft, which my sisters and I have sworn to obey. We've promised to draw on our gifts to protect our sacred spaces, to challenge skin-walkers and keep them at bay. We should never, under any circumstances, use our craft to casually kill any creature or person unless we're forced to; never use it to scheme, impose our will on others or dabble in darkness for money. I know this by heart, see. Nana drummed it into me from the beginning. Again and again, when she's teaching me at home, she's told me how things should be. Yet I'm still young enough to believe that some rules are flexible – a piece of string I can twist and tie according to my will. The truth is, I want Lance to like me so much, I don't care how many rules I break. If I can only feel the trace of his smile on my face once again, I'll be in blackberry heaven.

So, when Nana Merrimore calls me for lunch, after I've told her about Adoma's invasion of bats and she says, 'Trickery and death. Skin-walkers are on to us…' even though Nana's still in the room, I can't resist doing what I'm not supposed to. I adopt the qualities of another creature for my pleasure. In secret I take on a name so close to mine that I'm sure Nana won't notice; won't sense a shift in me.

'Linnet, dear Linnet,' I whisper at our kitchen table. 'Hide me in a charm of linnets.'

Bracken hisses while Nana stares at me. Then, touching her cheek as if sensing a kiss of betrayal, she watches my features shimmy and shift like the skin of a frog in a cloud forest. Nana gasps. And while my features ripple, allowing me to try on a new self for size, the cat vanishes.

'Linnet, dear Linnet,' I hum. And cloaking myself in another 'me', a prettier, more likeable 'me', a 'me' Lance will relish for ever, I glow in her colours of cream, pink and black. My cheeks shine, my hair radiates night.

Nana watches me hug my shawl tighter. She watches, as later that evening, I shelter in its feathery warmth. Next morning when I wake to find it gone, I get out of bed and look out of the window. There, floating on the lake's surface, is a small bird; its neck broken, its body entangled with strands of black hair.

I rub my fingers over my scalp and pummelling it

find a bald patch, round as a penny, by the crown of my head. I slam a fist in my mouth to smother my scream.

Anxious to scoop the bird out before Nana can see it, I scramble downstairs. But Nana is waiting for me.

'Linet, my dear,' she says, 'we need to talk.'

She sits down, takes my hand, and with her other hand lifts my chin until I can't help but look at her. Hazel eyes flecked with green douse sparks of anger in mine.

'Linet,' Nana says, 'you're not surprised by what's happened, are you?'

She lifts my chin a second time: 'Listen to me. Hear me well. What we teach you isn't for you. You do understand, don't you?'

I nod – a half-hearted nod maybe – for she goes on to say: 'If you insist on making this all about yourself, others are going to get hurt. You summoned a linnet, now that linnet's dead.'

Nana lifts my chin a third time and flinches at a flush of rage on my face – rage at causing harm and being found out. That doesn't put her off though. No, she clasps my hand tighter still.

'What we teach is for a greater good. I showed you that chameleon ruse because there are times when women of our sort have to blend in. Times when you and your sisters will need camouflage. It's not a trick to draw attention to yourself, quite the reverse.'

I bite my lip to soothe my indignation. Bite my tongue to silence it, keep the sharpness in. It shoots out anyway: 'Nana, all I want is Lance Gribble to *like* me.'

'Lance? Have you taken leave of your senses, Linet? There's a threat in the forest, a threat to all of us, and a pimpled boy is all you think about?'

'Lance isn't pimply!'

'Why pick Lance when you have your sisters? They adore you.'

Through gritted teeth, I hiss: 'My sisters aren't *here*!'

'All you have to do is call them and they're with you.'

'I want a proper friend on the moor!'

Nana gives me that look of hers. The look that says: 'I thought you were made of sterner stuff than this, girl! I thought you had mettle.'

'I like him, Nana, that's all. I want him to like me too.'

My grandmother sighs, shaking her head. 'There's no need to use deception, child. If he likes you, he'll let you know.'

'What if he doesn't?'

'Linet, don't stumble into the thicket of thorns your mother did. Don't break my heart a second time.'

'What happened, Nana? Tell me. I'm old enough to know now, aren't I?'

'Maybe you are.'

Nana folds my hands in hers, and looking me straight in the eye she says: 'What if I told you that your mother gave herself away too easily and lived to regret it? And then when you came along, she just couldn't cope...'

'So she left me.'

Nana nods. 'Your mother asked me to look after you, to hold you close and watch you grow. I've done my best.'

I'm about to ply her with questions when Nana deflects them the way she always does. She pulls me between her arms, scooping me up in a bear hug. 'You're the child of my heart, Linet Merrimore, and you always will be.'

She hugs me, holds me, and then puts me down, saying: 'Now, remove that bird from the pool. Bury it and wish it well.'

I step outside in my nightdress and run past an old rhododendron bush. The moment she hears me, Bracken meows, wriggling out of her hiding place. She sniffs my bare feet and satisfied I'm who she thinks I am, and not the imposter who frightened her yesterday, she nips my big toe.

'Have you missed me?' I caress the velvet fold of her ear, the moist kiss of her nose.

Bracken rubs her chin on my fingers, and follows as I run to the Linet Lake.

Nana Merrimore once told me that because of the work we do, the lake, an oasis of clean water for wildlife in a swathe of moorland, hasn't changed for hundreds of years. After what I saw in star time yesterday, I wonder how much longer we have before the damage filters through to here.

My daily task is to be a companion to the lake and honour it, while Nana receives visitors who consult her on herb lore and infertility, divination with cards as well. Mainly, she delivers babies. Delivers them in pools of water as she did me; then treats them if there's a need. A baby doesn't feed and fails to thrive? Parents bring her to Nana. She knows how to entice them to eat, how to identify minerals they have a craving for. Nana massages and manipulates their limbs. Stretches and flexes them to help them grow. First she deals with the babies, then she sets to work on their parents.

Whatever she does, it didn't work with my mother. Even so, Mama returned home to give birth to me. A week later, she dipped me in the lake's water and bathed me. According to Nana, I yelled. So much so, that Mama dipped her finger in the lake, and when my mouth was wide open, wet my tongue to give me my first taste of water.

This morning a light breeze ruffles the lake's surface. It whispers in reply and the dead bird, nestled on a dock leaf at the water's edge, drifts from the shore.

The lake beckons, and hands raised, I acknowledge my namesake:

> *'Linet-pool, Linet-pool, cool as morning dew,*
> *Your Linet-girl is here to play with you!'*

The water's cold today, the air above sharp and fresh.

I gauge the lake's mood through sight, sound, touch and smell. As a sweet scent of mulch settles in my nostrils, I take a first step to retrieve the floating linnet. All I have to do is grab it, then I'll bury it before Nana has time to cook breakfast.

A flurry of water curls around my ankles and the dock leaf drifts beyond my reach. It slips away as an insistent tug draws me in, until my shins are covered, the hem of my nightdress wet. The lake anoints me and stirs with birdsong. A faraway curlew calls, a sedge warbler chuckles, while choruses of blackbirds and thrushes fling reels of laughter in the air. I wade in.

The deeper I go, the further the lake nudges the dock leaf and its cargo. It's pulled to the middle of the lake, close to the circular whirl where women used to be drowned. It's the most menacing part, a roiling, dark place with an eddy so strong it sucks everything in.

Nana's told my sisters and I that even though at times our work can be perilous, while we're young, we're not to face danger alone. I know this and yet, because of what I did yesterday, I realise I've crossed a line. I can't change my name without a bit of a backlash. No one understands as well as I do how much words matter. They can soothe and heal, sting and wound, making the strongest of us bleed. That's why I'm convinced that the lake is testing me, teasing me.

> *'Linet-lake, Linet-lake, do you doubt my*
> *devotion?'*

A cluster of waves lap and loop around my waist as the lake lavishes me with kisses. I'm in deeper still, until I'm barely standing on tiptoe.

Bracken starts mewling. Whiskers bristling, she clamours at the water's edge. When I ignore her, she screeches loud enough for Nana Merrimore to hear.

I plunge into the water and swim closer to the edge of the drowning pool than I've ever done before. I swim and the lake lifts me in a loving embrace. Underwater weeds murmur at my shins and stroke my thighs. They lap against me, pressing me forwards.

My right hand grabs the dock leaf and wraps the bird in it. Then, with both feet kicking, I try to push my way back to the shore. I lunge, but my feet, knees, legs, my entire body, flails.

I dive underwater to break the current's grip. Cough, splutter, dive again, but the eddy is stronger than I am. It slurps, sucking me in until all I can see above is a dazzle of luminous sky through water.

'*Hukaa!*' my heart cries. '*Sisters, sisters, help me! Or I shall die in the pool of my Linet Lake.*'

On the slope of a mountain in the Gobi desert, Zula, herding sheep, stops, while Adoma, on her way to school in Ghana, slips behind a kiosk. Eyes closed, they focus, listening.

'*Sisters, sisters, tell the Linet Lake to have mercy on me!*'

'*Let go!*' my sisters say. '*The lake won't harm you. Let go, Linet-girl! Let go!*'

Easy to say, much harder to do. But with our hearts beating as one and their fingers entwined in mine, I'm able to smooth creases from my mind. As my thrashing limbs relax, a final thought blooms: *Mama, I never knew you, now I never will.*

Lungs aflame, the thought wilts. In that instant, when the only way out is to sink to a silty grave, the dock leaf in my hand twitches and a circle of hands pokes me. Around my ankles and feet, the prod and push of bony fingers shove me up. Hair swipes my face. My eyes open and gape. So this is the reason I'm not to venture this far. There's no escaping this watery tomb, for after all these years, through tempest, drought and flood, fragments of them are still here.

Where once there were eyes, I see sockets, and below cavernous holes gurgling. Light shimmers, particles of bone take on flesh, and faces emerge. Around me, a host of women: women dressed in sackcloth, solid one moment, next pale and insubstantial as ash. This isn't a trick of light in water. The witches who drowned here remain.

Among them, closest to me, is one whose smile reminds me of Nana's. Her smile tickles my soul and as her bony finger touches my forehead, the memory that haunts me unfolds. Only this time I see what happened. My mother's face ripples above mine while she holds me down. I struggle to breathe, to live. Behind her, Bracken spits.

The finger touches me again, and a jolt of electricity pulses through my body propelling me from water into air. The linnet in my hand bursts free, and as it flies away, I tumble to the ground.

6

Linet

When I come to, Nana Merrimore, alerted by her cat, is kneeling, her hand around my wrist. Bracken clambers over my legs. I splutter. Nana sighs – a long, slow release of breath that makes me realise she's been tracking my pulse. Fear burns bright on her face. So bright it might have frightened me at any other time or place, but I'm alive, aren't I? My sisters answered my call and in testing me the lake has confided its secret. In my left hand, I'm holding a purple, heart-shaped stone, a hole in the middle.

'Are you all right?'

I sit up gulping air. 'The bird…'

'It's gone,' Nana says.

Lifting me to my feet, she helps me back to Carbilly where she runs a hot bath in which she sprinkles oils of lavender and clove. My nightdress already in the bin, the stone on a window ledge, Nana plonks me in the tub and scrubs me clean of my adventure. My toes and nails free of grime, the slime on my legs brushed away, Nana towels me dry. She touches me slowly, tenderly while I wait for her fury to erupt.

I feel it whenever she touches me: coiled rage. And with each caress a crush of emotions I find hard to untangle. Emotions pumped by relief, which increase as she dabs behind my ears, my neck, my belly. She touches me as if she needs to know that every bit of me is intact.

When Nana's satisfied that I am as clean as I ever can be, she cooks me a breakfast of porridge sprinkled with nutmeg and cinnamon. Porridge followed by a slab of Spanish omelette. We eat in silence, Bracken, a warm curve of tenderness at my feet, while Nana's fury simmers.

She pours herself tea, then as an afterthought, offers to treat me to a bowl of hot chocolate. Its delicious aroma wafts through the kitchen settling in every nook and cranny of our home, beading the windows with droplets of steam. I watch Nana, her hand stirring a wooden ladle, as she slowly adds milk to melted chocolate. I watch and tremble at what I think I see: Nana's rage smelted into a strip of steel sharp as a Samurai sword.

She gives me the chocolate and sits down.

She doesn't wag a finger at me. She doesn't need

to. Not Nana Merrimore! She leaves me churning in misery until I begin to wonder if her anger will peak before I break. Should I say sorry first? Surely, she'll have to say something eventually?

Just when I'm about to stand up and scream because there's no way I can endure a moment longer, Nana says: 'You are never, ever, to do that again, Linet, you hear?'

'Yes, Nana.'

'You could have drowned. I've told you time and time again, you are *never* to go anywhere near the whirl of the pool. I've told you and yet you did! Why?'

I try to explain. I try to tell Nana that I had, in fact, remembered her advice. Not only that, Bracken warned me not to venture deeper too. I do my best but my stab at truth fails to convince.

An eyebrow raised, Nana frowns, and my voice draggles to a whisper.

'The lake insisted!' I say. 'I couldn't help myself.'

'So now you're telling me you had no choice in the matter?'

I nod.

'And your sisters? Did they know what you were up to?'

'I asked them for help, Nana, and they came.'

Nana shudders, shaking her head.

'They told me to let go. So I did. And then...' I hesitate, puzzled by a new expression on my grandmother's face. She gets up to clear the table.

Her back to me, Nana says: 'Go on, Linet. Tell me what happened!' Nana turns, hazel eyes searching mine for an answer: 'What are you keeping from me, child? Did you see something?'

'Nana, why are you frightened? I'm fine, really, I am!'

'What did you see down there, Linet?'

I could pretend that nothing unusual took place this morning, but instinct and loyalty to my sisters pushes me in another direction. If you can't be open with your teacher and guide, who can you be true to? Certainly not yourself! That's what Nana says.

So I ask: 'Haven't you seen them, Nana? The women at the bottom of the lake. Haven't they told you? Mama tried to drown me...'

Blood drains from Nana's cheeks as a palm slams over her mouth. When she's stopped trembling, she says: 'Go on, Linet...'

'They're still there, Nana, and among them is someone who looks like you. Her smile reminds me of yours... When she touched my forehead, I saw what Mama did.'

Tears slide down my grandmother's cheeks. She brushes them away and opens her arms. I run to her and she draws me in, swaying from side to side, while I cling to her.

Nana, my anchor, my lifeline, my teacher. I hug her. As she weeps, I sweep strands of silver hair from her face, and use the same words she does when I'm distressed: 'It's going to be all right, Nana. Nothing's ever as bad as it seems. Nothing. Absolutely nothing. And that's a promise.'

Nana sniffs and dragging her fingers through her hair, pulls it up with a clip. 'There!' she says. 'If there's one thing I want you to remember, no matter how events unfold, it's that your mother wasn't herself when she tried to harm you. Unhappiness unhinged her. That's why she left you with me.'

'She won't come back, will she, Nana?'

'I don't think so.' Her hand in mine, Nana sits me down. 'From what you've told me, I think what you saw in the lake this morning was the ghost of Hester Merrimore. Old Hester was one of us: a sharp-tongued truth-teller, the first woman in the parish to be accused of witchcraft and murdered for it.'

Nana shrugs as if that's all there is to it. But there's more, I can tell. A shadow lurks behind her eyes. She can't look at me, can't meet my smile.

'What is it, Nana? Whatever it is, I want to know.'

She shakes her head, then relenting, sighs. She repeats the action – a single shake of the head – again and again until grudgingly, she says: 'Very well, if you insist.

'You may not like what I'm going to tell you, child. There's always more to seeing a ghost than meets the eye, Linet. There are rumours and stories to consider as well as *how* that person died.

'As you can imagine, Old Hester's drowning wasn't the easiest of deaths. Her friends and neighbours, encouraged by the local priest, tied her up in a woollen sack and threw her in the lake out there.' Nana jerks her head in the direction of the drowning pool.

'As Hester started to sink, a sign in those days of her innocence, the witnesses present held back. They wanted to be sure, you see, certain that she wasn't in league with the devil. They waited too long. By the time they hauled her from the water and out of the sack, by the time they'd pummelled her chest and tried to breathe life back into her, Old Hester was dead.

'She was innocent. Cleared of witchcraft, yet for ever remembered for crimes she didn't commit. That's how it is with Merrimore women. The gifts the lake gives us, gifts we practise daily and nurture, put us in harm's way.'

Nana might have left it at that, if it wasn't for a smell emanating from the pores of her skin.

'Nana, why won't you tell me what's the matter?'

She bends over, kisses the top of my head and smiles her special smile, a smile as surprising as a cat's lick of sunshine on a winter day: 'Rumours and stories, child,' she says. 'It's nothing to worry about, but people used to say that once a Linet-girl has seen Old Hester's ghost, it's more than likely that the oldest Merrimore alive will soon join her. That's what they said a long time ago.'

It takes me a few seconds to grasp what she means – seconds for my pulse to quicken, my head to swirl. 'You don't believe that do you? Tell me you don't. *Please.*'

She gives me that special smile again.

That's when I ask: 'Are you going to die, Nana?'

7
Adoma

✴

When Linet called us a second time that day, I was with Milo, a rescue monkey I look after, watching a match on Ghana television: Asante Kotoko versus Accra Olympics. It was half-time and our emblem, a porcupine, was up against theirs: the Olympic flame with its five rings. Kotoko supporters were jumping up and down, doing the Kotoko jig, because we were halfway to thrashing Olympics three nil. Yah-yah! I was singing our song, when I heard Linet's call: '*Hukaa!*'

I'm used to being summoned. After all, I do my fair share of summoning myself: when it's dark and I want to speed through the night sky somersaulting with my sister squad; when I want to chat long and hard about what we're learning and how our gifts are growing, I call them, 'cause I'm a sucker for sister-magic. But to be called twice in one day, a cola at my side, eyes scanning the television in case the game started again, now that was difficult. What's more, I was at a friend's house: my one and only true friend, Kofi Agyeman, the boy I shall marry when he admits I'm as fast as he is at football – sometimes faster. I should know, because we practise dribbling and tackles whenever we can. I'm the dribble princess of our village, a future contender for the Black Queens, while Kofi has set his heart on playing for Chelsea. My One and Only has big dreams – oh! 'Poor on earth, a loser for ever in heaven,' he says. So what better way to learn about football than by watching our team on TV? It's not every day Kotoko meets Olympics. But then it's not every day that I hear *twice* from my *O broni*, my white sister, Little Linet.

'*Hukaa!*' she called again.

'*Chale*, I have to run,' I said to Kofi.

He screwed up his face in disgust: his nose, his eyes, all of him. 'Adoma, how? When we dey kill those Accra boys? Noooo! If you want to be my girl, you go stay!'

'Your girl? Kofi, I'm one hundred per cent my own girl, you have no idea!'

'Then I beg you, stay.'

'Girl talk!' I flashed my phone at him and ran outside, Milo following. Quick-quick, I had to find a place to talk with Linet.

I live in a ramshackle village a good distance

from Kumasi, capital of the Ashanti region. My grandfather, Okomfo Gran-pa, likes to say that Kumasi is the garden city of Ghana. Didn't see any gardens last time I was there. But hey – this be Ghana – oh! And in my broke-down village we've learned to make do with the little we have. Poverty snaps at everyone's heels, here. It gnaws at the belly, gobbling up sleep when on market day, there's no money for food, no money at the start of a new term to pay school fees. We live by the sweat of our brows, we do. We have to.

Linet called late in the afternoon when farmers were on their way home from their plots, cutlasses sheaved on their shoulders, and women and girls, heads laden with firewood, hurried down a track that passes as our main road.

A tumult of sound came from every compound. *Thump! Thump!* Wooden pestles hitting mortars. Fufu pounding: heavy, monotonous, up and down. The whole wide world and his wife were getting ready for an evening meal of fufu: boiled plantain and cassava, pulverised into a round ball and wolfed down with soup. *Boom! Boom!*

The noise spoke to me saying: 'Adoma! Girl, you're hungry! Cola no be food!'

Another voice whispered: 'Adoma! Instead of wasting time watching television with Kofi, you should be at home helping Gran-ma like a "good" girl.'

I sniffed, disgruntled. Now, if I were a boy, no one would expect me to stop roaming and stay put. Believe me, I'd be allowed to play football at every street corner and do exactly as I please. No problem!

I scampered to our house on the outskirts of the village and entered round the back, through the open kitchen where, sure enough, my grandmother was pounding and turning fufu on her own. She looked at me, eyes dark with reproach.

'I'm coming,' I told her and fled to my corner of home before she could call me back. Before she could shout:

'Adoma, that monkey-child of yours is not to go in the sitting room! Come back!'

Gran-ma's command echoed behind me. Thankfully, I was already inside. I slammed the back door and could no longer hear her. Perfect.

What I call my 'corner' is in an alcove of the main room of a zinc-roofed house that my grandfather, Okomfo Gran-pa, built years ago. Gran-pa's a priest. A traditional priest, by which I mean a Before-The-White-Man-Came priest, when most people behaved differently. A woman couldn't have a baby? She consulted Okomfo Gran-pa. Perplexed by the burden of a family curse? If you visited my grandfather, depending on the potency and longevity of the hex, he might be able to help you.

Gran-pa built his house before I was born. Even

so, when I tumbled into the world, he made space for me. I sleep on a raffia mat behind an ancient sofa his father bought at the time of Ghana's independence. Our Freedom Day sofa is still wrapped in plastic, a sign that only the most important people who come to the house are allowed to place their backsides on it. As usual, Milo leaped on Old Freedom and like a true man about town, stretched out, laying his head on one of Gran-ma's precious pink cushions.

Under cover of dusk, I sat on my sleeping mat and rubbing the *nsoromma* tattoo on my wrist, opened up to my sister-friend's summons: 'What is it, Little Linet?'

I sensed her agitation as soon as she burrowed into my mind. She'd been crying. Zula, already with her at our sanctuary in the forest, was doing everything in her power to calm her. Even so, a sob escaped.

'Hush,' Zula said. 'There's no need for this.'

Linet snuffled and all I could feel and hear as I joined them was the violent heaving of her chest, like a crushed pair of bellows unable to inhale air. She made an effort to control herself – an attempt shredded by tears.

'What is it, Little Linet?' I asked. 'Has Bracken been bitten by a snake? Is there a problem at the lake?'

We were in shadow, able to see without being seen at the river goddess' shrine. Trees pared of fruit in star time still flourished here. There were no dangling bats visible, no sign of the slither and hiss of catastrophe I'd sensed the day before when I'd spoken on the phone to Gran-pa in Accra. After he'd consulted with our teachers, he confirmed what Zula had said. Bats were an omen that skin-walkers were on the prowl and could attack us anywhere, at any time. They were coming.

A cool breeze whispered through the leaves of the hardwood trees that formed the outer rim of the glade. Sap still surged under bark, heartwood strengthened, stretching, while underground, tangled roots untangling signalled to their neighbours. I kindled a fire with a spark from my finger to silence the hum of mosquitoes.

'Bracken's fine,' Linet replied. 'I'm not worried about her, but my grandmother. She's going to die.'

She sobbed, lip-swollen-heart-breaking sobs. 'And another thing – I discovered today that I drove my mother crazy when I was born. Nana says her hormones ran riot and she tried to drown me. If it hadn't been for Bracken howling for Nana, I wouldn't be here.'

She shuddered. Our minds merged and as the three of us became one, Linet's tears trickled down my cheeks as well. I wiped them away. I'd often wondered how it was that although she lived in a brick house with a tiled roof in the country that had colonised mine, Linet was always under siege, beset by storms of emotion that held her captive. Now I understood. It's bad enough to have a mother who doesn't want you, like mine. But to have one who tried to kill you was too much. Within seconds, all three of us arrived at a place beyond language in which a sequence of images unravelled.

What we saw was: Nana Merrimore washing Linet in a tub, Nana Merrimore cooking breakfast and afterwards asking what Linet had seen at the bottom of the lake. Threaded through the pictures like shadows on the sun were ghosts, one in particular. I peered, trying to make out a face. Next moment a mighty blow slammed my chest as if someone had hit me with a fufu pestle.

'If there's one thing I want you to remember, it's that your mother wasn't herself when she tried to harm you,' I heard Nana Merrimore say. Then: *'No, Linet, I'm not going to die.'*

The old woman held and caressed my sister-friend, soothing her through words and touch. But no matter what Nana Merrimore had said, Zula and I detected the tear in Linet's heart, and felt the agony of it.

'What should we do?' whispered Zula.

'Only a fool knows exactly what to do in a crisis,' Okomfo Gran-pa would say.

'Don't know,' I replied.

'Take your time, Adoma.' Gran-pa again. 'Think before you jump into a river strong enough to sweep an elephant away.' Gran-pa, the shrewdest man in our village, the head of our family business, the shrine to the goddess that protects us and other villages upstream.

I took note of his advice as another thought came to me: a hunch accompanied by an image of a deep, dark well of water. I looked down the well and called Linet's name. An echo rebounded, boomeranging in a jangle of noise that petered out in a whimper. Little Linet is lonely and feels lost, I decided.

What would Gran-pa do to ease her pain? What words would he use to take the hurt away? Gran-pa's wisdom rustled through my mind, awakening my own, while Zula, thinking along the same lines, recalled her grandmother's good sense.

'Grandma says that what a baby chick sees in the nest it repeats when it grows up. Nana Merrimore is your nest, Linet. Your grandmother, not your mother. Even when you've learned to fly, Nana will be in you and no one living or dead can take her away.'

Zula spoke and words tripped off my tongue into our circle: 'Linet, whenever you need us, we're with you. We're lucky because we're never going to be alone, us three.'

Huddled in a ball, Linet wiped her nose on a knee. 'That's easy to say, but the truth is I feel more cursed than lucky, and I don't ever want to leave my nest.'

'I've got your back, my sister,' I replied, remembering days when I'm like that: in a melancholy mood. Days when my mother's home, and after scolding me, unleashes furious prayers over me. Days when Gran-pa and my mother argue, when she condemns what we do at the shrine as *ju-ju* and then Gran-pa says: 'As for you and your Holy, Holy religion, have you ever wondered how the white man made us follow him? How he made us believe in his ways and in so doing turned some of us into skin-walkers as well?'

I remembered days when everything tastes sad, days during the rainy season, when my spirit, bitten by mosquitoes, is sick with fever.

Under the circumstances, all we could do, Zula and I, was to hold Linet close. We did. We held her, warmed her and then watched as the wound she was nursing sprouted into a garland of thorns that circled her heart.

'One day soon, my nana's going to die,' said Linet. 'When she goes, I'll be alone. And they'll put me in a home somewhere.'

'Don't you have relatives you can go to?' asked Zula.

'Nana Merrimore is all I've got in the world.'

'Except for us,' I stressed, recalling the many moments we'd shared together: the hours we'd spent perfecting the delicate skill of listening before speaking, the knack of observing, the art of intuition and herb-lore.

And Linet? Though the lake flowed through her, it appeared to haunt her. The image of the well rose in my mind once again and resonated in Zula, for after I'd dipped a finger in its water, she did too. It chilled us to the bone, this place of loneliness in our sister.

I tried to imagine what it must be like to have no relatives to speak of. Not to know where your mother was, the name of your father. Though I lived with my grandparents because my mother didn't have time for me, I knew where she was and the name of the man, who, having planted his seed in her womb, wanted nothing more to do with me. According to Okomfo Gran-pa, after my birth my mother had wanted a fresh start and so he and Gran-ma had taken me in. Yet I had cocoa sacks of aunts and uncles and cousins; so many, in fact, that whenever I started counting them, before I could finish, another cousin had been born and I'd have more to add to my list.

'But isn't Nana Merrimore healthy?' asked Zula.

Linet nodded.

'If she's healthy,' Zula went on, 'she has every chance of living to a great age.'

Linet sighed, then said quickly before she could hold back her words: 'I saw the ghost of Hester Merrimore this morning. She gave me this.'

Linet opened her hand to reveal a small, purple stone with a faint sparkle of amethyst.

'This is a truth-teller's stone,' said Zula, touching it. 'It will protect you. Wear it as a talisman,' she instructed, closing Linet's hand.

Linet tightened her grip. 'In her heart of hearts, Nana believes that when a Linet-girl sees Hester's ghost the oldest Merrimore alive doesn't have much longer to live. I can't change what she believes, so the odds are...' She moaned, pressing her palms to her eyes to stop her tears.

I held her: 'No one knows what's going to happen tomorrow,' I said. 'Up one day, down the next. Anyway, what about Lance?'

'Seek him out,' Zula pressed. 'Befriend him.'

Linet wasn't so sure: 'Who will take my side when Nana's gone?'

'*We will*,' said Zula and I.

'But,' I added, 'your grandmother's still alive and might be for a long time.'

'*Adoma!*'

Gran-ma. Gran-ma called a second time, and this time her anger slashed the silky cocoon of our circle.

Linet trembled. Her shiver, rubbing against me, reminded me of the frightened, lonely child I become after one of my mother's tirades, a child with the knowledge that not all mothers are good because some are dangerous and wage war on their children.

I'm sure Zula sensed it too, for what I remember is that Zula blinked and from a pearly grey eye a teardrop fell.

8

Adoma

✳

'Adoma! Adoma! Where are you? Ha! Asleep again!' Gran-ma squeezed her lips, kissing her teeth in disgust. 'I've never met a girl who sleeps as much as you do! Are you feverish?'

I said goodbye to my sisters and turned as if protesting at Gran-ma's intrusion.

She continued shaking me: 'You'll soon be a woman, my girl. You won't be able to sleep as much then!'

I yawned to extinguish a smile. And then like someone clinging to sleep, I pulled away from Gran-ma.

'Gallivant, that's all you do,' she grumbled. 'You're either playing football with Kofi or roaming the streets like a stray goat.'

Gran-ma continued whipping me with her tongue. She assumed I'd fallen asleep on my mat, a mistake I chose not to correct. That she claimed I was idle suited both of us. I could slip away whenever I pleased.

Besides, as a diviner, who placed pebbles and water from our sacred river in a pot to peep into the future of her clients, if Gran-ma *pretended* she didn't know what I was up to, she couldn't be accused of being a follower of the craft. Old women can be lynched in seconds here, while a child of the sky, a warrior like me, can escape by running like the wind.

'Adoma, get up! I'm not here to wait on you!'

Faking drowsiness, I rubbed my eyes and slowly got up from my mat. Too slowly as it turned out, for by the time I was standing, Gran-ma's attention had shifted to Milo.

'Just look at that monkey creature of yours! Get off my sofa! If I see you on Old Freedom again, I swear on all the gods in Ashanti, I shall put you in my cooking pot. I shall butcher you and eat you, chop-chop!'

She shooed him away. He sprang into my arms chattering through bared teeth.

This chimp understands language, I tell you! He knows who to trust, who to fear and realises that as long as I'm around, no one this side of the equator, not even Gran-ma, would dare harm him. He knows this, because until he's old enough to fend for himself, Milo is my responsibility. Milo also appreciates that due to her liking for 'bush' meat, Gran-ma could never be a true friend.

'Shush,' I said to soothe his chattering. 'She's only teasing. Aren't you, Gran-ma?'

A short, round ball of a woman, skin the colour of nutmeg, eyes black as coal, Gran-ma winked at Milo.

'If you stay off Old Freedom,' she said, 'you're safe from my pot. You understand?'

Milo buried his face in my shoulder.

'Well?' said Gran-ma. 'I'm waiting for an answer.'

I nodded on Milo's behalf.

'Good,' Gran-ma said. 'We now understand each other better than husband and wife. Adoma, come and eat.'

❧

Two days later, when Gran-pa returned before daybreak on a night bus from Accra, having already told him about the colony of fruit bats that had invaded the goddess' shrine in star time, I shared an incident that pestered me.

'Last night, Gran-pa, between waking and sleeping, I changed.'

He looked at me. Still in his travelling clothes: khaki-khaki shirt and trousers, he was eating a crust of bread for breakfast.

'I changed,' I repeated. 'I was not as you see me here, Gran-pa, but newly made into a queen of the forest at our shrine.'

He beckoned and then touched the tattoo on my wrist. Straight away he saw what I'd seen and sensed what I'd felt. On padded paws I'd slunk through undergrowth and jumped up a tree. Claws gripped bark before muscles sinuous as silk draped on a branch. A cool breeze whispered through the leaves around me. Behind me, the silhouette of forest foliage loomed, looping in wolf-light, while quiet as a ghost, I watched with eyes that weren't mine and listened, ears pricked.

'I was a stranger even to myself, Gran-pa, yet I knew it was me, because the trees in the forest: leaves, roots, bark, heartwood, sapwood – *everything* – whispered my name.'

Gran-pa nodded, moving quickly, urgently. 'Something's happening, Adoma, and we need to be there.'

Since time was of the essence, Gran-pa decided that instead of walking to our sanctuary, which would take an hour and a half at least, we should travel on his scooter. We set off with me sitting behind him, Milo swaddled like a baby on my back.

My grandfather held the firm belief that early morning is the best time to begin a journey. The sun was already up, the first blush of its light soft and gentle before the harsh sting of high noon. The air was cool as we careered out of the village down a dirt track pitted with mounds and stones. Gran-pa knew the path well, and by twisting and turning his motor, avoided damaging its tyres. We sped along, Gran-pa greeting farmers and labourers on their way to work, while I waved at women cooking by the roadside, my age mates ambling to school.

Once our village was behind us, farm plots gave way to the lush green vegetation of ancient palms laden with flowering creepers. On we rode, following meandering paths through neighbouring villages and farms, until we approached the edge of the forest – a protected area for animals, birds and trees.

Gran-pa brought his scooter to a halt and dismounted. I followed him. I put Milo down and slung a rucksack on my back. It contained, among other items, water and a midday snack of boiled yam and fish. I trotted beside Gran-pa, while Milo scampered ahead into the forest where he'd been discovered beneath the body of his dead mother.

'Not so long ago,' Gran-pa said, 'all of this was deep forest. A forest so dark you had to carry a lamp to find your way through it. They cut the trees to build the village back there. First came the village, then villagers slashed through virgin forest to grow cocoa. And before long, they destroyed more trees to make charcoal for their women's cooking pots.' He tut-tutted, shaking his head. 'Now they wonder why the rains don't come with the same vigour as before. They wonder why the land is drying up and the air is dusty.'

Gran-pa strode into the undergrowth, along a path I'd memorised when he first brought me here, years before. He followed the route I take when I attend to the river goddess' shrine, when I dance for her and bring food to her. Milo raced ahead, and when we passed a giant silk cotton tree surrounded by an orchard of wild bananas, he clambered up a trunk and swung from tree to tree whooping with joy. Further on, a grove of towering mahoganies was marked with red paint – a sign that someone intended to cut them down illegally.

'Open my bag, Adoma.'

I did as I was told and removed a plastic bottle of paint remover and two sponges from the rucksack. I handed the bottle and a sponge to Gran-pa and with the other copied what he was doing: wetting the sponge and swabbing off the paint first from one tree, then a second, until one after the other the entire grove was clean of paint. This is what we did every time we came to the forest – saved as many trees as we could from destruction. It was, after all, a protected area, but from our experience of protecting trees from harm, I understood that in Ghana rules didn't apply to everyone.

The job done, I followed Gran-pa's example and tramped from tree to tree, stroking the bark of the first, crouching at the gigantic roots of another. As he touched and caressed the huge plants, so did I; and in the same way that he did, I sensed them. Even more so, when Gran-pa began chatting as if to old friends:

'Who knows if this will do any good,' he said to a mahogany so tall that the simple act of stretching my neck to glimpse its crown made me dizzy.

'It may fool our enemies for a week or so,' Gran-pa went on. 'Maybe a fortnight, if we're lucky. But in the end they'll put their mark on you again and cut you down. Those devils have no respect for a tree as venerable as you, comrade.'

As Gran-pa patted its trunk, and proceeded to the next, I did the same. I didn't talk to trees though; I simply touched them, alert to the foraging of their roots, the hiss and whisper of leaves, as one tree gestured to another. As I listened, a colony of blood-orange glider butterflies drifted from the canopy and flitted about my face.

'Between breath and feather, scales and wings,' I murmured, 'talk to me, friends, tell me what you've seen.'

A few settled on my head, while others dusted my eyelashes and cheeks with their paint, before landing on my arms and legs. The agitation of wings and whirl of antennae spoke even louder than the trees. My heart leaped.

'Gran-pa,' I said. 'We may be too late...'

I brushed the gliders away with a waft of wind from my hand. It carried them to where Milo rootled in the canopy. Suddenly he stopped. Still as a sloth, he cocked his head, uttered a bark, and scrambled to the safety of my arms.

'Someone's coming, Gran-pa,' I said. 'Let's hurry to the shrine.'

'No,' he replied. 'I'm too old and tired to play hide-

and-seek. This small piece of forest is protected. They shouldn't be cutting down trees and they know it.'

'Are you sure, Gran-pa?' I was getting ready to run to avoid a confrontation that could turn ugly. But there was something else, a sense of disaster rumbling in my ear that the forest was alive to.

'Stay, Adoma,' my grandfather said. 'All will be well.'

I put Milo down, grabbed Gran-pa's sponge and stuffed it in the rucksack with the paint remover.

Reminded perhaps of his mother's murder by poachers, Milo scrambled up a tree taking refuge in its branches. In the distance I heard the footfall of men walking towards us. Every few steps they paused to slash creepers. I heard the sweep of a machete, then the tear and snarl of vegetation trampled underfoot.

'Two men,' Gran-pa said. 'Two strangers.'

I nodded. They had to be strangers. Only outsiders with no idea of where the track was would attempt to hack their way through the bush.

'Hide,' I whispered to Milo, up in his tree. 'There's still time to leave, Gran-pa,' I added. 'Nothing good's going to come from these strangers. We're needed at the shrine.'

He shook his head and stood firm.

Okomfo Gran-pa was my teacher and guide and yet, observing him that morning, I was startled at how old he appeared. His gaunt face glinted blue-black when sunlight, glimmering through dense leaves, danced on his skin. His eyes darted and delved to the heart of everything around him while he stood, his back to a tree.

The seam of unease I'd felt moments before, refused to disappear. What set me on edge were sparks of defiance reflected in my grandfather's eyes: that, and a growing presence of danger that a shadowy creature inside me, a creature with paws and a leonine head, signalled by clawing the ground.

As the footsteps advanced, I moved and stood slightly to the side of Gran-pa to better protect him. It's much harder to harass an adult with a teenager in tow, than an old man alone.

A machete cut through the undergrowth and a policeman, tangled in tree vines, fought his way into the clearing. In a holster he carried a gun. A few metres behind him was a corpulent, middle-aged man with a handkerchief in his hand. The fat man mopped slicks of sweat off his brow as he struggled to catch his breath. The armpits of his shirt were stained wet, its white print flecked with the trail of snails and pollen.

'I thought it was you and I was right,' the policeman said.

'Is this the man?' asked the fat man.

'Indeed, master. Okomfo Gran-pa is well-known for his loving-kindness to trees.'

Gran-pa stood up straight. 'Do I know you?'

The policeman, a young man in a dishevelled

uniform, three thin scars running down the side of his face, smirked at a secret joke only he was aware of.

'Sir,' he said. 'I am Inspector Kaku from Kumasi. 'I've been staying in the village back there with my friend here.' The inspector nodded at the fat man.

The fat man was wheezing, still trying to catch his breath. From what I could tell, he wasn't used to walking; and certainly not walking and talking at the same time.

'What can I do for you?' asked Gran-pa.

'You, old man,' the policeman replied, 'are giving me a headache. A severe headache that not even paracetamol can quell. Why do you keep doing what you shouldn't be doing, old man?'

A flicker of amusement passed over Gran-pa's face. 'What am I doing that I shouldn't be?'

'Sir, are you laughing at me?'

I held my breath as the policeman's fingers fluttered and then touched his holster.

The fat man tapped the younger man. 'Inspector, let me do the talking here. Okomfo, allow me to introduce myself.'

The man walked towards Gran-pa, his right hand outstretched: 'Mr Ebenezer Lamptey of Save Our Trees for Ghanaians Incorporated.'

Gran-pa folded his arms to make it clear he wasn't interested in the usual formalities. Instead, he stepped sideways, legs astride.

I reckon I would have done the same too, for underlying the upturned curl of the man's lips and the sleek smile in eyes magnified by glasses, was the distinct odour of corruption. It seeped out of him making the air around him rank with the stink of rotting fish. The man was most probably a liar as well. Gran-pa Okomfo knew it and so did I, because the closer he came to us, the more my skin crawled and the more physically ill I became.

That's the way it is when a skin-walker approaches me. Their lack of human kindness is so distressing it knocks me off balance. Skin-walkers have no heart to speak of and no soul as far as I can tell, because they're after one thing: money. And the dirtier it is, the more people they flatten to obtain it, the better it makes them feel.

The smile fixed on his face, Mr Lamptey withdrew his hand, allowing it to dangle by his side. 'Hostility can have dangerous repercussions, be careful, old man.'

'I am always careful,' Gran-pa replied.

'Not careful enough, it appears. According to the villagers, you're in the habit of removing marks off trees my men designate for timber. Your stubbornness is costing me money, old man. Unless you stop your foolishness...'

I moved to stand directly in front of my grandfather. 'Are you threatening Okomfo Gran-pa?'

The fat man ignored me while the policeman laughed – a hearty belch of glee that doubled him over until, clutching his stomach, he ended up giggling like a schoolgirl.

'I asked you a question. Are you threatening my gran-pa?' I managed to keep my voice level, calm. I was merely a teenager to the world, but Gran-pa taught me long ago that when danger arrives the only way forwards is to face it squarely with eyes fixed on it.

Mr Lamptey was now about ten paces away. If he didn't reply correctly, if he continued thinking that I was a small girl he could dismiss out of hand, in another three paces he would feel the full force of my fury in the form of wind magic.

Puzzled by the wry smile on Gran-pa's face and the ferociousness on mine, the fat man froze. A smile greased his lips again; a smile that didn't reach his eyes. Yes, he had the eyes of a skin-walker, all right, the eyes of a dead man walking.

Mr Lamptey harrumphed and said: 'Let me make myself clear. My men mark the trees and the final product, the furniture we make, ends up in the homes of our fellow Ghanaians. What is your problem with that, old man? It be our wood, we be Ghanaians, we dey chop!'

Gran-pa raised himself to his full height and pointed an accusing finger: 'Mr Lamptey, I may be old, but I'm not a fool. Not so long ago we even had rangers who patrolled the forest. We both know that these trees are protected.'

Ebenezer Lamptey shrugged and then nodding in the direction of the policeman said: 'Protected? Protected from what? This is Ghana, old man, and I have the law by my side. So, unless you stop making our lives difficult...'

His chin jutting out at Gran-pa, Mr Lamptey came a step closer. He took another step, examining me as if inspecting a toad he was about to obliterate with a stamp of his foot.

'Unless I stop making your life difficult, you will do what?' Gran-pa replied.

No one said a word and for a couple of seconds no one moved. Even the leaves of the trees we'd saved seemed to stop rustling as the birds nesting within them ceased singing. All of us, every living thing present, waited for Mr Lamptey to complete his threat. The police officer touched his holster. I tensed and the hairs on the back of my neck stiffened as I prepared to harness wind energy within and outside me. We waited and as we did so, I inwardly begged Mr Lamptey to come a little bit closer. A step, just a step, would do.

He took it and when he did, I was ready. No one speaks to Okomfo Gran-pa like that and gets away with it. I balled my mind into a tight fist and like a boy with a sling, released a single stone in the mighty arsenal I possess: nuggets of concentration packed with sharpened flints of power buoyed by air blasted the fat man's chest. *Zing!*

'Aie!' he cried. 'Aie!' Screaming, he toppled to the ground, a hand clutching his ribcage where his heart should have been.

Unnerved, the twitchy young inspector lifted his firearm and fired it above his head.

I was on the verge of repeating my mind blast, when Gran-pa signalled that I should stop. He wanted the man to live.

'Help me,' Mr Lamptey groaned.

Gran-pa knelt beside him. The policeman did too, while I stood and watched.

'Easy...' Gran-pa straightened the fat man's head and torso to make it easier for him to breathe. 'Don't talk,' he said. 'Inspector, run to the village and get help...'

Crouched beside his accomplice, the policeman asked: 'Master, should I go?'

The fat man moaned, gasping for air.

'Go!' Gran-pa repeated. 'Your master cannot talk. Run, man! Run! Round there, it's quicker. Adoma, give Mr Lamptey some water.'

I opened our rucksack and knelt down, pushing a cup of water to the fat man's lips. His bulging eyes, shiny with fear, shrank at my touch. He would have spat if he could, but he needed water. He gulped it down and as he started to recover, Gran-pa spoke.

'Do you hear the forest talking to you, my friend?'

A dove cooed in one of the hardwood trees that had been marked for timber. Another bird replied singing an octave higher. The dove cooed again and in the hush that followed a rush of wind whistled through leaves.

'Do you hear the forest?' Gran-pa asked.

Instead of replying, Mr Lamptey closed his eyes and grimaced. He placed a hand on his chest.

'The forest is alive, my friend,' said Gran-pa. 'It watches and waits. And to those who desecrate it, it reserves a punishment worse than death. The forest has warned you, Mr Lamptey. Don't cut down any more trees, you hear? Because next time you do, your end will be near.'

9
Adoma

That my grandfather knew much more about the inner-workings of the forest and how its eyes, ears and breath affected each of us was only to be expected. Indeed, it was Gran-pa who'd explained to me years before, that what I'd believed was an unusually vivid dream – my first encounter with Zula, Linet and Zula's father over the Sleeping Giant's mouth – wasn't a dream as such, but an example of night travel perfected by our craft.

That's when he revealed the symbol on my wrist. He raised my hand while he touched the middle of my forehead with a finger.

'Can you see it now?' Gran-pa asked removing his hand from my wrist.

'What? I thought I was dreaming, Gran-pa!' On my wrist was the symbol Zula's father had made:

nsoromma. It had been there all along but I hadn't been able to appreciate it. 'Why couldn't I see it?'

'Not all your eyes were open, Adoma. Now that they are, can you see mine?' Gran-pa held out his arm. On the inside of his elbow was an *adinkra* symbol of a bird, its head turned backward taking an egg off its back. 'The ancient wisdom of *Sankofa*,' Gran-pa explained. 'A return to our roots to learn from the past. Every member of my circle carries this symbol.'

'Why isn't yours the same as mine?'

'Our circle is a foretaste of what is to come.' Okomfo Gran-pa smiled to ease the confusion on my face. 'We turned to the past to revive old ways of working with earth and sky. We're teaching you what we've learned, so that when the time comes you and your sisters will find new ways to prevail in our battle against skin-walkers.'

'How will we do that, Gran-pa?'

'When you're ready, you'll know,' he replied.

It took almost an hour for Inspector Kaku to return. Almost an hour during which Mr Lamptey avoided looking at me. Even though I gave him water and helped him sit up, he sensed that something I had done, something he couldn't see or put a finger on, had, in one way or another, hurt him. I'm not sure which upset him more: the thought that a 'small girl', a girl he wouldn't normally bother to look at, had crawled under his skin and bitten him, or Gran-pa's stern warning to stop cutting down what was left of the rainforest.

On his arrival, the policeman organised his helpers – two men from the village – to carry Mr Lamptey in a fireman's lift to safety. As soon as they set off, I called Milo down from his hiding place. I reassured him that all was well, and we continued our journey to our river sanctuary.

Okomfo Gran-pa was forever saying that the forest is a living being that uses trees for its lungs. Everything within it is alive and should be treated with the utmost respect. If you're about to cut down a tree to use its wood, before you do so, you should ask the tree for permission. What's more, the forest is blessed with millions of eyes and ears. Those hidden eyes stalked us as we walked, and those ears listened while we talked. I felt them. And yet with every step we took towards the clearing where our shrine stood, I had the distinct impression that a forest that usually welcomed us with the unruly chatter of birdsong was ill at ease. Those butterflies had prepared me.

Even so, I wanted it to be me that was off balance, me who broke the spider's web of dread spinning around me. With the sun high in the sky, humidity at ground level was beginning to sap my strength.

Our early morning start combined with a sponge-like clamminess in the air made me limp as a wet rag. This is what I wanted to believe. But the further we walked, the more I began to realise that it wasn't only me who was on edge, but the forest itself.

Tell-tale signs of disturbance flickered wherever I looked: broken stems, crushed leaves, and where the earth was exposed, marks on the ground that indicated a scattering of Colobus monkeys and wild hogs. What had caused such a stampede away from the river? I wondered, as from moment to moment the forest revealed clues: bruised petals of orchids, dangling fronds of a battered palm. Most uncanny of all, an eerie silence prevailed. There was no noisy swooping of ibises overhead, no tussle of animals in the undergrowth and not a whisper of air in the trees. Even Milo seemed alarmed by the sultry, claustrophobic stillness.

I looked up at Gran-pa.

'You feel it too, Adoma,' he said.

I nodded. 'Zula was right and so were you. Those fruit bats were an omen. Hurry, Gran-pa. Hurry.'

I was trying to imagine what lay ahead of us when I heard the river that cuts through our sanctuary. What should have been torrents of water was little more than a trickle. I listened intently, aware of other noises now. Voices. Many voices behind the chug and whirr of machinery, the slip-slop of buckets filled, then emptied.

Gran-pa stopped, his finger to his lips. We slowly advanced aware that what had previously been thick forest had thinned out. Indeed, thickets of trees, which should have continued for at least a thousand metres before opening out to the river, came to an abrupt halt at five hundred. Rows and rows had been felled. All that remained were broken trunks scarring the air like the ravaged stumps of an army of amputees.

Instead of an intricate web of branches and roots, sticks and leaves to hold the earth in place, from the edge of the forest to the river was an excavated field of muddy, red silt. The river had been diverted by machines and dammed into rivulets that spilled out over acres. The water was soggy, filthy. Nothing could survive in that. And, for the foreseeable future, nothing would grow on that sea of sludge. Nothing could breed in it, because apart from teams of young men and women panning water in basins, everything was dead and dying. Supervising the teams were two Chinese men wearing long rubber boots.

'*Asemane*!' said Gran-pa, a hand on his mouth. 'What have they done? What are they doing?' He looked on in horror and as he did so, I was struck by the rapid throb of his pulse beneath his open shirt. His heart was breaking and so was mine. For what he saw and felt rebounded in me. Tremors of pain, similar to what I'd experienced through Linet a few days before, shook me. Only this time the ache was stronger and my confusion so profound that it was as if the fabric that held my life in place was being ripped apart. The river goddess hadn't heard my call. Every bit of me shook at the stench of death in the air and my failure to protect our sanctuary.

Yet the people on the riverbed didn't look as corrupt as Mr Lamptey. The Ghanaians, especially, didn't resemble skin-walkers in any way that I could remember. They were people I knew from our village and the hamlets around it. Ordinary people, most of them older than me, among them faces I recognised. Junior, the son of our chief, was chatting to a tall, Chinese man, then relaying his orders to the people around him. More buckets were filled with water. More of the river was diverted. If they had any idea of the damage they were doing, they hid it well.

'Look at them, Adoma!' Gran-pa said. 'They're searching for gold! *Galamsey*! And the chief's son is with them. If they find gold will they be able to eat it for food and then drink it for water? How will their parents farm now? How will they find water for their families?'

Too shocked to form words, I held my tongue. The shrine I'd tended for seven years had been trampled. Desecrated.

'They're poisoning the river,' he said. 'What they're doing here is going to destroy the country and kill every one of us in the end. Foreigners may not care, but have we forgotten what we're about?'

All I could do was nod. Pain and anger flamed in my marrow, while in my heart a creature buried within me roared. The image of a leopard flashed through my mind. If she had her way, she would rip the throats of everyone present and devour them. I wiped my tears as upstream and downstream, the trees that still remained seemed to move as one. They swayed, releasing a sigh that a breeze swept into a sky in which vultures circled. While on the riverbed young men and women laughed.

10

Zula

✳

That night, I summoned my sisters to the Giant's mouth where Adoma described what she'd witnessed by the river. She spoke haltingly, her pauses punctuated by gasps and sighs that Linet endeavoured to ease by saying: 'Go on, Adoma. Go on.'

When Linet's coaxing was met with silence, she poured words into the mix: 'It's unbelievable,' she said. 'It's like, if I were to wake up tomorrow, step in the lake and discover that the water in it had turned to mud. Surely those people understand they're hurting themselves?'

'Grandma says it's only when people are given time to taste the bitter fruit of their deeds,' I replied, 'that they begin to learn from them, like my Uncle Batu.' At the mention of my uncle's name, his tale of unhappiness in the city burrowed like a weevil in my mind.

Adoma remained quiet. Bereft of language, she stared blankly at us while we each held her hand. I teased her fingertips and as I touched her, pictures of what she'd endured unspooled. Linet shivered. She too saw what Adoma had witnessed. And she too felt Adoma's shame at having failed to protect the river and forest.

'I should have spent my nights there,' her heart murmured. 'If only I'd been present when they arrived, maybe I could have stopped them.' Her eyes wet with tears, Adoma hung her head in despair.

'It's not your fault,' said Linet, touching the stone Old Hester had given her. It dangled from a string around her neck. 'What else could you have done? You and Okomfo Gran-pa could have been killed if you'd got in their way.'

I agreed. The trick, as Pa would say, was to live through misfortune, learn from it and then act decisively. Those fruit bats had indeed been a warning that the balance of our world was askew. But now that our sanctuary in the forest was gone, what should we do?

'Okomfo Gran-pa says that while we're learning the tools of our craft, we must be patient,' Adoma's heart answered with a sigh.

'That's what Nana Merrimore says,' Linet confirmed, 'as well as your grandma and pa, Zula.'

I nodded. 'They've taught us well. We know what we believe in. We are for the earth and the sky.'

Taking up my cry, Linet added: 'We are for every creature that walks and crawls on land. Every creature that flies in the air or lives in water.'

Adoma's pulse quickened.

'We are children of the sky, sky-warriors,' I said. 'Protectors of the earth, determined to do our best by aligning ourselves with *nsoromma*. Take heart, Adoma! We may have been defeated this time but one setback does not mean the battle is over.'

I leaned forwards and as my forehead touched theirs, my sisters and I swayed in silent communion.

Outside our den, a September gale surged, hammering the rocks around us with sand. The squall blasted everything in its path. Dark clouds rolled over the cave, somersaulting through the fir trees below. As the branches creaked, the trees bent to the tempest's tune. The seasons were changing. The heat of summer was giving way to cooler autumn days, while high in the mountains at the Sleeping Giant's mouth, nights already cold were becoming colder.

Linet trembled. Her brow against mine, her new talisman glowing, I saw a bird hatch within her. The chick tumbled from its shell and opened its wings, stretching. A tiny feather fluttered on to my lap, while in Adoma, I saw a leopard break free. I suppressed a growl and pulled away.

Right now, simply being a friend to Adoma was what mattered most. Little by little, as the wail of the gale soothed her, her thoughts settled, and after her tongue lost its numbness, Adoma described what had happened next at the river.

'Milo wouldn't let go of me,' she said. 'I had to carry him on my back, while Gran-pa Okomfo was so distraught he could hardly walk. The shrine in pieces and the river, the sacred river, the source of life to us, destroyed.'

'We hurried back to the village to speak to the chief – a relative of Gran-pa's. I never knew that Gran-pa had so many words rattling about in him. How he talked and argued and talked some more. We were in the chief's palace by then. Gran-pa had poured libation, so that the ancestors would be present to hear everything.

'"Listen," said Gran-pa. "The least we should do in this life is make sure that what the ancestors left us, we pass on to the next generation. And to think that your son, Junior, is working with strangers to spoil our river. The goddess of the river will not forget it."'

Adoma quivered, a flicker of memory closed her eyes. Teeth gritted, she opened them again: 'That's when the chief smiled. A fat, greasy *boflot* smile. An I-feel-sick-and-need-to-burp smile. Too much sugar in the dough, too much oil in the frying pan. His lips twitch, I tell you. Then he calls a small boy. Asks him to fetch a pouch. The pouch on his lap, the chief opens it and hands Gran-pa a wodge of money. Plenty money. Money enough to feed us for three years. And Gran-pa? He won't touch it. "Nana Chief, what do you take me for? You forget, I was your prefect at school…"

'The chief repeats his *boflot* smile. He urges Gran-pa to forget about our shrine by the river and concentrate on the one in the village instead – the one in our backyard. He should put it all behind him, the chief says, and chop small. Gran-pa shakes his head this way and that. No, he won't. He can't. Now the chief orders him, commands him to take his share. When Gran-pa insists that he won't touch a pesewa of the chief's bounty, Nana Chief says: "Okomfo, I advise you not to become a thorn in my flesh. If you do, I shall be forced to pull you out and throw you away."

'Gran-pa could sense the hair at the back of my neck bristling. Quick as a mosquito about to bite, he catches my eye and blinks to tell me "no". He could sense what I wanted to do: blast the man to the next world and plunge thorns in his feet to stop him returning to planet earth. Gran-pa squeezes his eyes at me, gets up and we leave without saying a word.'

II

I am wolf.

That night after I return home to our ger sleep lulls me. I'm running with a pack of she-wolves. The biggest of them twists and turns through a sea of feather grass, moving like a white streak on the steppes. In wolf-light the grass glistens pink and gold, reflecting the last of the sun as it slips from the sky.

Stretching my legs, bounding as quickly as I can, I catch a whiff of gazelle and whine.

The biggest wolf turns sharply and her dark, amber eyes pierce mine. 'When we hunt as a pack silence is our friend.'

She signals to the she-wolves and changing tack, they start circling our prey. I run ahead, eager to be in at the kill.

'Back!' the biggest wolf warns me.

I freeze. Instead of a gazelle, an enormous brown bear lopes towards me. I snarl. Hackles rise. About to charge him, a heave from the biggest wolf shoves me aside as she shoulders the brunt of the bear's blow. Fangs bared, the pack lunges, and one after the other savages him.

They rip out chunks of flesh, chunks of fur and gristle. They snap at legs and knees. The bear keels over and the pack pounces at his neck, tearing it open. Blood seeps into the steppes; and as the wolves eat, their leader at my feet gently licks me.

12

Zula

My soul journey felt too vivid to be a dream. Combined with Adoma's anguish, it troubled me, digging in my mind, dirt in my eye. Dirt that I couldn't remove or blink away, niggling at me as darkness gave way to light.

I described my night travel to Grandma as she stirred a cauldron of stew she'd cooked for breakfast. She listened, prompting me with questions about the colour of the bear, its size.

Once she'd heard what I had to say, Grandma frowned: 'Your quest was about much more than you, Zula. Did I ever tell you that Little Bear was my nickname for your Uncle Batu?'

I shook my head. Hardly anyone in our family mentioned my uncle if they could help it. And when they did, it was to use him as an example of how not to behave.

'Batu means *loyal*,' said Grandma.

The suggestion that my uncle hadn't lived up to his promise dangled between us as the weevil inside me tunnelled out. 'What happened to him?'

Grandma sighed, stirring the pot. 'My last-born was going to be a shaman. When he strayed, when he turned his back on us, he lost his wits.'

Grandma slapped her thigh, and her del, a calf-length garment fastened at the shoulder, quivered.

'But isn't my uncle better now? Pa seems to think so.'

'So did I until you told me what you saw in your night travel, Zula. A twisted tree cannot straighten itself easily. But this I do know: skin-walkers are coming and so is your uncle.'

'But it wasn't real, Grandma!'

She handed me a hot bowl of food, holding it so I was forced to attend to her words before eating. 'In the same way that they've destroyed Adoma's sanctuary in the forest, skin-walkers have their eyes fixed on the Giant's mouth.'

'No!'

'Remember the rumours we heard earlier this summer? Rumours about miners who plan to dig into the Giant's belly to search for copper and coal?'

'That's not going to happen yet! Pa said it would

take years for our politicians to decide what to do. And before they decide, they'll let us have our say.'

Grandma snorted. 'Politicians don't listen to people like us. Believe me, my winter wolf, for the sake of earth and sky, we must prevail.'

A few days later, Grandma began coughing. Grandma was frailer these days and when she took ill, all of us – Ma, Pa, my brothers, my uncles and their families who lived close by – paid particular attention to her.

Within a half-hour of her cough starting, Pa dipped into his medicine box and brewed a sweet tea of honey and ginger for her chest. From noon to late afternoon, the cough dogged her, so that with every tickle in her throat her innards heaved, until she was forced to take to bed breathless, complaining of aches and pains in her joints.

Next morning, after a sleepless night of Grandma's tossing and turning, Pa sent me on an errand in search of plants to heal her. I was to go across the steppes in the direction of the Sleeping Giant. There, on the slopes of the mountains, I would find the herbs he needed to soothe the fever raging in Grandma's lungs.

I set off on Altan, the horse Pa had given me years earlier on our return from our first visit to the Giant. I'd chosen him when he was a foal in Pa's herd, and

had named him after the sky the morning he was born
– Red Dawn.

I'd fed and watered Altan and made sure, when he
was old enough, that I was the one who rode him first.
By then he was used to me. So much so, that once I'd
lassoed him, I easily leaped on his back.

Altan bucked and whinnied. He wriggled, spun
around. I smoothed down flames in his mane, which
flickered like embers in wind. I dampened the blaze and
then gentled him by whispering his name and mine.

'It's me, Altan. It's me, Zula. Zula, your friend.'

Altan neighed, pawing the ground. He bucked
a second time, and then galloped over scrubland.
Grasses parted in his wake, lizards scuttled as his legs,
hitting their stride, thundered along the length of our
grazing ground.

Grandma has a saying that a Mongol without a
horse is like a bird without wings. In Altan I discovered
my wings and whooping with joy, I clung on. Within
minutes, my horse settled into a canter. And all the
while a westerly wind enfolded us, murmuring tales of
friendship between Mongols and their stallions.

On the second morning of Grandma's cough, a
day heavy with foreboding, Altan and I travelled at a
gallop. The morning sun hung low in the sky throwing
a ghostly shroud of light over the landscape. Pa had
made it clear that I had to find the plants he needed
quickly. Old lungs hot with fever, weighed down

by phlegm, can strip life away within hours. It can snuff it out as quickly as a blast of cold air can dowse a candle, Pa said. I didn't need further prompting to understand that Grandma's life was in peril. I set off determined not to let her down.

The landscape we rode over was alive. Larks flitted above shrubs, kestrels glided behind clouds, then swooped to catch snakes. For mile after mile, tall grasses flurried in the direction of a breeze scented with wild garlic. I breathed it in, and as the tension in me gradually eased, the sight of saxaul trees on the horizon told me we were almost there. Give or take an hour or so, Grandma would soon be better.

I was so convinced of what my heart longed for that my eyes were blind to warnings, which on any other day would have given me pause. The closer we came to the mountains, leaves and grasses were sprinkled with dust, I failed to notice. And I failed to take heed, a few moments later, of a hazy mist on the horizon.

My mantra was 'Grandma will soon be better. Grandma will soon be better.'

Altan slowed to a canter, then a steady trot as we approached the slopes of the Sleeping Giant. To my left were the beginnings of a birch forest. I directed Altan straight ahead up the steep rise of the first hill. On our descent the other side of a rock-ribbed slope, a bright colour caught my eye. It blinked at me. Blinked and then winked.

I dropped from my horse and scrambled to take a closer look. Yes, it was one of the plants I was looking for: a late flowering gentian, a cluster of blue bell-like flowers at the tip of its stem. I removed a knife from my side pouch and dug it up, carefully teasing it out of its moist home: roots, leaves, stem and flowers. I placed the plant in my pouch.

By my reckoning I'd been away from home for about two hours. All I needed to do now was to find the fruit and leaves of a juniper bush. I clambered on to Altan again and was riding down the hill, when I noticed a caravan of trucks snaking along the ravine of the Sleeping Giant's mouth.

Just then I spotted a juniper bush in fruit. In the distance the caravan rumbled on. I was plucking and placing berries in my pouch, when an explosion rang across the valley. Boulders and dust flew in the air. Birds dropped from the sky. A spray of sand and pebbles erupted. The detonation was so powerful that as its sound reverberated across the mountain range, bounding off great slabs of rock, the earth shook, knocking me off balance.

I tumbled onto my bottom as Altan reared. His hooves dangled above my head. I knew he would do all in his power not to harm me, but even so instinctively, I rolled.

Round and round I spun, faster and faster down the hill. Head, body and feet gathering dust, while a squall embedded with soil from the other side of the valley powdered my clothes and skin. And still I rolled until I used both feet to halt my descent.

I sat up, spluttering. Five minutes later, Altan found me. He nuzzled my head and, urging me to stand, prodded my back.

'I'm fine,' I told him watching the caravan, sand whirling from its wheels, wind its way to the bottom of the valley.

I couldn't believe my eyes. What were they doing over there? Why had they blown away a side of the mountain so close to the Giant's mouth? What if they were going to destroy him completely? Was it in our power to stop them?

For a moment I forgot Grandma. All I could think about was the place I visited and summoned my sisters to in wolf-light: the Giant's mouth. I saw the wings and talons of the eagles that nested there, heard the baying of wolves that serenaded me when in winter rain and snow, or on parched summer days, I made the journey to break bread with the Giant and sing to him. The more I lulled him in slumber, the more he became a part of me: blood, breath and bone. The deeper his caves and crevices bedded in my soul, the deeper my love for him. I'd loved him since my first taste of drizzles of honey and horse's milk at seven years old. I knew the crags the Giant lay on as well as I did the lines on my grandmother's face. If outsiders came and destroyed even the tiniest part of the range, they'd destroy me as well.

I raged, incandescent at the possibility that Grandma was right. What if what we'd thought was rumour wasn't tittle-tattle but fact, and companies from outside already had permission to mine the mountain? But then why hadn't we been told? Why hadn't we been given a chance to have our say? But then if Grandma was right...

I wiped dust off my face and clothes and climbed back up the hill to complete my task. I quickly collected the rest of the juniper and stored it in my pouch. An image of a she-wolf flashed before me.

'My winter wolf! Where are you?' she cried. *'Come home, winter wolf! My eyes want to see you one last time.'*

'Grandma!' I gasped. 'I'm coming. Altan!'

My horse came to me and we set off back to our pasturelands.

My legs tightened around Altan's flank. Lengthening his stride, his hooves strummed the ground as his canter stretched into a gallop.

'Faster, Altan. Faster,' I shouted and he obeyed. He galloped as never before and with his muscles rippling like wind across the steppes, we returned home.

13

Zula

I jumped down from Altan and flung myself through the door of our ger. Inside was hushed, the only sound the murmuring of Pa's prayers over my grandma.

'No,' I cried. I was too late. That's what I believed, until I reached Grandma's bed and saw she was breathing. 'I'm here, Grandma,' I said.

Her eyelashes fluttered and in my mind's eye, she turned midway on her journey to the stars, to wave goodbye.

'No, Grandma, don't go! I've brought your medicine,' I told her.

I handed the plants to Pa. He shook his head.

'Please, Pa! I know you can save her.'

Pa shook his head a second time, but now that

I was home surges of adrenalin and hope made me defy him.

'You're going to get better,' I said to Grandma. 'You'll see.'

Her eyelids spasmed. She moaned and after what seemed a great effort, opened her eyes.

'You see,' I said to Pa, elated. 'Help her!'

He did as I asked. Perhaps it was Grandma's smile that stirred him, her raised hand as she reached to touch mine.

Within the hour, he'd produced a concoction of gentian to ease the heat in Grandma's lungs.

I helped her sip the medicine and then held her hand as she curled into sleep. I watched her, willing her better, willing the gentian to do its healing work. To do it well, do it quickly. I watched and listened. Her breathing was shallow but the colour in her cheeks was better. They weren't flushed any more. I touched her wrist. Her pulse, though weak, was steady.

I stayed by her side that night. And to keep her warm crawled into her narrow bed and slept with my arm wrapped around her bony shoulder. While Pa worked over the stove in the centre of the ger, making a balm of juniper to ease the pain in Grandma's joints, I slipped in and out of sleep.

In those moments betwixt and between, when I was not fully awake and yet not quite asleep, my mind revealed images that had eluded me in the day's drama.

That haze of dust on the horizon; dust like a shimmer of silk on the leaves of plants. How could I have missed it?

If it hadn't been for my grandmother, I would have woken up and mentioned the dust to Pa there and then. I'd have talked about the trucks I'd seen that afternoon and the explosion in the mountains. If I hadn't been preoccupied, willing Grandma to live and listening for gaps in her breathing, Pa and I would have talked about how best to protect the Sleeping Giant.

I was focused on Grandma alone. Would she survive the night? And if she did, how many more days before her spirit took flight?

I recalled what I'd said to Linet at the prospect of Nana Merrimore's death. I'd used Grandma's words, Grandma's wisdom. Those words came to me again in the voice I knew so well: '*What a baby chick sees in the nest it repeats when it grows up.*'

I understood Linet's reaction better now. Even though I had family around me and would never be as isolated as she was, I too wanted my grandmother to live. I wanted her here. Present. Always.

Pa often said that every living thing is spirit in earthly form, and in the end each and every one of us returns to the home we came from. I knew this and believed it. And yet the mere thought of Grandma's death rendered me breathless.

I placed my face close to hers and with my hand on her chest followed the pit-patter of her heart. Our breath mingled, the rise and fall of my lungs moved in rhythm with hers until exhausted, I fell asleep.

❧

I dreamed that night that I was a baby swaddled in my grandmother's arms. Grandma, her dark mane of hair flecked with grey, gently rocked me as she sang a lullaby:

> *'Little winter wolf,*
> *Stay warm, grow strong.*
> *When the moon shines in the afternoon sky and*
> *wolf-light is nigh,*
> *We turn to wolfish ways and stay in the long*
> *grasses of the steppes.*
> *Follow me, my grey-eyed cub,*
> *Come and play with our sister wolves today.'*

Grandma sang, and her face held me transfixed. I luxuriated in it, drinking it in. Her head tilted tenderly towards me as the red embers of the stove danced in her eyes. Love radiated from them. Love, which I guzzled like a thirsty horse does water.

Grandma sang her song to me and in the blink of an eyelid we were outside in wolf-light. My hands and feet became paws, the hair on my skin grew matted, enfolding my body in a blanket of fur – the dazzling white fur of a winter wolf. Grandma turned into a huge she-wolf while my ears, nose, mouth and teeth changed into those of a young adult. With her nose nuzzling mine, our bodies lurched and twisted while we danced in the late afternoon sun.

A feather tickled my memory. 'Grandma, this has happened before, hasn't it?' I said.

'All the time,' came her reply.

'I remember fragments as in a dream.'

Grandma licked a space on my forehead just above my eyes in the place Pa says my third eye resides. She touched it with her tongue and all at once I saw and remembered not just snatches of our time together in wolf-light but *everything*: moonlit summer evenings spent running with the wind; early mornings chasing my tail in dew-drenched grass and hunting – the joy of the pack.

Memories flooded through me and I lapped them up: the deft manoeuvring of the chase, the heady rush of capture, and finally the kill. Fangs in fur, a sharp shake to break the neck, then a feast of meat and blood. My grey eyes flashed diamond at the thrill of it.

'This is who you are, Zula,' Grandma said. 'This is part of the gift you've always had: this, and your love for the man in the mountains, the Sleeping Giant. Tell your sisters, my winter wolf, that until the three of you use every morsel of what's inside you, we shall never defeat today's skin-walkers.'

Shadows lengthened in the dream, bringing a new scent that Grandma picked up: the odour of a fleet-footed hare. Eager to pursue it, she said: 'Come with me, Zula, on this my last hunt. Follow me.'

I ran after my grandmother. She rocketed ahead and stopped. When she turned, a hare dangled in her mouth. This she gave me and as I tore its flesh into pieces and wolfed it down, Grandma spoke in the lilting voice I loved:

'Be brave, Zula. Be fierce and have no mercy on those who would harm us and obliterate the sacred places we revere. I see with my wolf's eyes that changes are already in motion to destroy you and your sisters. First they will annihilate your mentors, teachers and guides. They've done for me, for it is their dust that has hastened my end. They will come for your father. Be vigilant, my winter wolf. Farewell.'

'Wait, Grandma! Wait.' I wanted the dream never to end. I wanted her voice to continue talking, singing, laughing. 'Another lullaby, Grandma,' I pleaded. 'Sing to me.'

I tried to keep her with me, tried to grab her and hold her close so that she wouldn't go. But dreams have their own magic, their own rhythm and purpose. I knew, even as I begged Grandma to stay a while longer, that when I woke, her body next to mine would be cold.

14

Linet

A blanket of heat shrouds thorn bush and scrub, sucking moisture from soil.

The haze thickens, but before a drop of rain falls, a breeze blows it to sea.

Parched earth cracks and hardens. Woodland and forest wither. Rivers shrivel and die, even as mansions spring up to touch the sky. The sun scorches until a moment comes when tinder sparks.

Flames crackle, torching trees while embers whipped by wind spill over canyons, bounding from hill to hill on to the roofs of houses. Buildings ablaze, those covered in skin, feather or fur burn.

Turkey vultures, hyenas of the heavens, hover, their hisses smothered by the rumble of thunderclouds. The sea swells, the earth sizzles on fire.

In a faraway forest a leopard dances to the moon.

While on the moor, as soon as the plume of a bird tumbles into a girl's hand, an invisible wing flexes.

'No one said life would be easy, did they?' This is what Nana Merrimore has taken to saying.

She said it when I told her about Zula's grandma, how devastated Zula is by her death, how unhappy I am at losing a teacher.

'Nana, Zula almost died in that explosion!'

I got the usual response.

Only last night when we'd talked about the carnage at Adoma's forest haven and I described how the sacred river running through it is now bloated with floating fish, Nana faithfully repeated those words. *'No one said life would be easy, did they?'*

It's her method of conveying that not only is she as hard as Cornish rock cake, she's mighty tough as well. Merrimore tough: a proud descendant of the first woman in our parish to be drowned in the lake, a woman whose gift of a purple stone, I now wear around my neck.

And so what if I've seen Old Hester's ghost and have made her token my talisman? Is Nana Merrimore spooked? Of course not! She's already put it behind her. She's as wiry and resilient as an old bristle hairbrush is Nana. Or so she pretends to be. And me?

I'm old enough to play along with her, see. To look the other way when she touches my charm and says: 'Old Hester's telling me it's time I went home, Linet. Time for the blossom to give way to the fruit and return to the womb I came from.'

I look somewhere else as she pulls out her Tarot cards, and after the Hanged Man crops up again and again, she turns to the *I Ching*.

I pretend not to notice when she can't catch her breath, and wonders if breathlessness is a sign of a dreadful something growing inside her. I've learned to pander to her pride by averting my eyes. Nana knows this. Even so, now my mother's tears no longer frighten me, she hasn't been able to be honest with me.

While I wait for Nana to unburden herself, I've taken to truth telling by the lake, Bracken curled on my lap. In drizzle-mist and wolf-light, I fondle the stone and ask the lake and those she shelters for help in teasing out my thoughts. Thoughts I'm wary of because of what's inside me. I feel it, hear it: a beak snipping at the cage of thorns around my heart, a bird eager to fly. It wriggles, tickling as it pecks a way out. There's the bird; then there's Lance.

This morning my cheeks flush as Old Hester reaches me in a voice soggy with peat and water: 'First you must learn to trust what's inside you,' she says. 'Learn how to talk to it and own it. Then sheath the mischief at the tip of your tongue and talk to your Lancelot. You can't stay scrumped up like a hedgehog for ever.' She laughs and a gurgling of bubbles surges from the depth of the lake. 'Give your gift a try, petal. You've nothing to lose!'

Later that afternoon I make my way across the heath. High on the moor are Cairns, stone burial grounds from long ago. A zephyr wind blows from them, reminding me as I walk below of the mumbling of ghosts and the rustling of trees that once stood there. Warm flurries spin about me whipping my hair with the remnants of leaves and twigs.

Between one step and the next, there's a chill in the air. The wind bites in a cold snap. I shiver. Feathers. I need a cloak of feathers to shield me from gusts meaner than winter on the moor. The thought seizes me and straight away I feel them: feathers down the length of my back, feathers around and about me until I'm swaddled warm.

I make my way, the squelch of peat underfoot, to a woodland grove in the dip of the valley by Crow's Nest. There, from bushes sheltered by trees, I pick blackberries, eating some before storing what's left in a blue bowl in my basket, a bowl pale as a bird's egg. Tongue stained purple, I follow the route I took days before.

'How be my sister-friend?' Adoma murmurs, tickling my mind.

'I'm fine,' I tell her. 'Just fine, see.'

'Are you on your way to see him?'

I nod, smiling.

'*Aba*! Your lips and tongue are stained black, my sister. Go home and wash! Brush your teeth. Is that a cloak of feathers you're wearing?'

'Can you see it?'

'Of course, I see it.'

'I wonder if Lance can...'

Adoma laughs: 'If he spies those feathers on your back, he'll run away faster than a flea from a slap!'

'That isn't funny, Adoma!'

Adoma chuckles, then disappears.

A swoop of swallows trawling in the wind's caul streams overhead. They hail me at the start of their crossing to Africa, or so it seems, for my heart quickens as I hear cries of: 'Linet-girl! Linet-girl! Help us travel faster!'

My right hand in the air, I assist them with the beginnings of a gale that rushes from my fingers. My hand wafts in the direction they're heading and they're away!

'Between blood and bone, breath and feather,' I call to them, 'travel well, my friends, to your journeys' end.'

When I arrive at Crow's Nest all is still. There's not a whisper of a breeze to disperse the scent of mulch and peat. I open the gate. It snarls, startling starlings on a pylon nearby. They take flight in a dance that unravels like a never-ending scarf. They swoop and retreat in welcoming chatter. Loop to peer at me, then swing their wings in a whirl that curls up into the sky until tumbling down they perch on the roof.

I knock. No one answers. I'm about to place Nana's bowl on the step, when the door opens and there she is: Mrs Gribble, my old babysitter. Eyes black as a raven's, her brow furrows, puzzled.

'How you've grown, Linet! Come in! Come in!'

I remember to smile just in time. 'This is for you, Mrs Gribble. I was passing...' I hand her Nana's bowl full of blackberries.

'Well, thank you! How are you and your nana, these days? Won't you come in?'

'Maybe next time. Say "hi" to Lance for me. And Arthur...' I add.

'I will,' she replies.

I turn tail and run, my cloak of feathers lifting me off the ground.

Next day there's a knock at Carbilly and I *know* it's him. I heard his footfall as he walked to the door, his cough before a scent of blackberries seeped in.

'I'll get it, Nana!'

I race to the door. Pull it open.

Lance is taller than me, and blushes as soon as he sees me. My cheeks flush in reply. In his hands is Nana's bowl filled with eggs. Chicken eggs.

I should call Nana.

I want to bolt. I bite my lip instead and stand tall; so tall I'm able to thank him before I place the bowl on the kitchen table.

As I turn, he says: 'I thought you were a ghost when I saw you in our yard. A ghost lost in mist.' His smile licks my skin once again, warming me inside and out. Wings outstretched, the bird in my chest flutters, singing.

'Do you have a bike?'

I nod.

'Fancy a ride up a tor and down again? I'll race you.'

I grab my bike from behind the shed, and we're off.

15

Linet

✳ ✳ ✳

On my return to Carbilly, I'm so dizzy with the fizz of blackberries on my tongue that my skin's humming. Body and soul are strumming so much that, about to open the front door, I pause, fill my lungs with air and as my heart soars, squeeze my eyes tight.

Inside I hear voices. They dip and disappear. An American drawl, clipped English rush, nipping and chasing until Nana interrupts.

Nana's tone is hushed, her voice low. So low, in fact, that I have to strain to hear her.

'Be discreet,' Nana says. 'I've notified my lawyer and she'll be in touch with you. I want everything signed and sealed in case we're forced to prepare for the worst.'

Nana pauses. I hear her draw breath, hold it, and then exhale.

Breath control – a technique she uses to keep her emotions in check. I imagine her clasping her hands, fingers and thumbs leaving indentations on her skin. Something's wrong, seriously wrong.

'Does the girl appreciate what's happening?' asks the American.

'You'll have to talk to her,' the woman says.

'I want to, but it's difficult. She's a child at heart. All of them are. Don't misunderstand me,' Nana continues, 'the three of them are exceptionally gifted. They've learned fast and mastered key elements of the craft already. They've acquired a sensitivity to touch, sight and smell that few possess. But in truth, we simply don't have the time to prepare them for what's coming.'

The American laughs: 'Zelda, sweetheart, is anyone ever completely prepared for what lies ahead? I doubt it.'

Grizelda is Nana's Christian name. Only her oldest, dearest friends call her Zelda. These strangers aren't clients then. Not only that, I've never heard anyone call her *sweetheart* before. I lean in and tiny follicles in my ears twitch.

'Nowadays, whenever I bother to take in the news,' the American goes on, 'I'm reminded of my father reading from the Book of Revelations. What I hear is a litany of fire and pestilence, drought and famine. And floods. Never-ending floods! It doesn't take much to connect the dots, sweetheart.'

'That may be so,' Nana replies, 'but now that

it's down to us and the young ones we've guided, I discover I'm paralysed. I can scarcely breathe at times.' Nana thumps her chest.

The hairs on my neck sizzle as the palms of my hands moisten with sweat.

'Zelda, how can we help?' asks the English woman. 'What can we do? Tell us and we'll do it!'

Nana replies and her panic, rising from deep in her throat, bleeds into me: 'There's a mighty storm coming our way and it's going to affect all of us. Much as I appreciate your willingness, dear, sticking a finger in the air isn't going to stop it.'

As if sheer determination alone can drag Nana away from an abyss she's staring into, the woman repeats her offer, only louder this time: 'If there's anything – anything at all you'd like from us – you've got it. What else can we do?'

Nana tries to talk but ends up moaning instead. Stutters and then pushes words into the open: 'What they're doing has already killed Zula's grandmother. Her father or Okomfo Gran-pa is likely to be next. Then it'll be my turn.'

This must be Nana the diviner speaking. I told you she's been leafing through the *I Ching* and reading Tarot cards to peep into the future.

'Are you sure?' The American again.

By now my ear's clamped to the front door. I'm desperate to hear Nana's reply, when Bracken, inside, rumbles me. She snuffles up my scent and meows. She scratches at the door, leaving me with no alternative but to barge in pretending I've just got back from my ride.

What I see in Nana's sitting room fills in the blank spaces of a picture I've painted in my mind. I'd hoped that the strangers were clients. Indeed, I want them to be. Anything but this confirmation from Nana's lips, of what Zula's grandmother foretold. Grandma said that she would be the first to go, then one by one our teachers would follow: Zula's father, Okomfo Granpa. Not Nana. Anyone but her!

I look away from my grandmother and take a deep breath in which I drain every trace of emotion from my face before I say 'hallo' to her friends.

Peering at me is a tall, giant of a woman with the dark, pebbled eyes of a crow. A smile flutters her lips.

'Hallo, Linet,' she replies.

The woman's skin is tanned leathery brown and her black hair, piled high on her head, is coiled in a mess that resembles a bale of fraying rope.

The American beside her is even taller. Dapper yet angular, his long limbs are folded and looped in Nana's largest armchair.

'Hallo,' says Nana. 'I thought you'd be out longer.'

'So did I, Nana.'

I'd wanted to run in and tell her, before I was waylaid at the door, that I'd made a friend. Tell her his name and then shout it out to the lake and the moor.

Now, overwhelmed by what I've heard, I recognise the paralysis Nana spoke of as a combination of numbness and awkwardness creeps through my limbs. It immobilises me, until I finger the stone around my neck.

Somehow, I make my tongue move: 'What's going on, Nana? Are you all right?'

Nana pulls back a strand of grey that's wriggled out of its clasp, and holds out her hand. 'Come here. Give your old grandmother a kiss!'

I touch her hand and wince. Nana's not ill as such but terrified by a sense of foreboding that goes beyond my sighting of Old Hester's ghost. This is worse, much worse.

I embrace her – not an everyday 'Hi there, Nana, I'm back from my bike ride,' kiss, but a heart-felt hug. 'What is it, Nana?'

My question is met with that iron curtain of secrecy I know so well.

'I couldn't help hearing some of your conversation...' I confess.

More silence. This time peppered with a rapid exchange of glances between Nana and her guests. If they've got a trunk load of secrets and want to hold on to them, there's no need to make it so obvious. Any one would think, the way they're behaving, I've as much sense as a two-year-old.

Bracken tries to jump onto my lap. I caress her head and as she nuzzles my palm, my thoughts return to Lance: his frankness, his offer to race me to the tor, our hectic cycle ride there followed by yelps of joy as we hurtled down. Just thinking of his candour makes it hard to hold my frustration in. I can't go on pretending that everything's fine, everything's as it should be, when I know it isn't. If there's any chance that I can make things better for Nana, then I must take the trouble to be as honest with her as I am with the lake and those within her. That's the trouble with truth telling. Once you start, it's hard to know where to stop.

'Nana, I don't think I'm frightened of dying,' I begin. 'Everything dies in the end. I know that. I just don't want to live in a world without you in it.'

Every mouth except for mine opens as their faces crumple.

Nana blinks away a tear, then glances at her friends. *You see what I mean*, her eyes seem to be saying. *You see what I'm dealing with here?*

'Is it true, Nana? Are you going to die soon?'

I've already admitted that I eavesdropped on their conversation. To me, it's as clear as the daylight outside that I need to know more. I have to. Indeed, I'm minded to invite my sisters. I'm on the verge of doing so, when Nana heaves herself up from her chair.

'No one's going to die,' she says. 'I'm certainly not ready to. Not yet, at any rate. But I do have something important to tell you.' She slides a finger down the curve of my cheek, cups my chin in her hand and then kisses my forehead: 'I was about to tell you. But before I start, I intend to get everyone a drink.'

'I'll do it, Nana.'

'No, I will. I need to stretch my legs.'

Nana bustles about in her drinks cabinet. 'What's your poison?' she asks the strangers.

'Whatever you've got,' the woman replies, 'will go down perfectly, Zelda.'

Nana traipses back and forth from the kitchen. Crushes ice. Pops open a bottle of fizz, then reappears with a tray of four champagne flutes filled with a sparkling pink liquid. Sloe-gin fizz, Nana's favourite cocktail.

'Would you like to try one today?' she asks me.

I nod. She hands me a champagne flute and passes the tray to her guests.

'Linet, I want to introduce you to some old friends of mine. Rosie, this is my granddaughter, Linet Merrimore. She looks after the Linet Lake out yonder. And this is Redwood.'

I smile at them. We raise our glasses and the three of them say with one voice: 'Here's to long life and the old ways. May the earth nourish and bless us each and every one. May the sun smile on our faces and the fair wind that blows behind us carry us safely to our resting place.'

While they make their toast and take a first sip of their drinks, I call on my sisters to come to hear what I'm about to be told. They surface in shadow, the contours of their limbs and features flickering about me. One moment by my cheek, as Adoma sits beside me, and the next, after I've drawn breath, by my feet where Zula settles.

No one else, it seems, can see them but Nana and me. Or so I think, until Nana's friend, Rosie, pauses, the champagne flute half-raised to her lips. She blinks and takes a hasty sip of her drink while she gazes at the lights glimmering around me.

Rosie's more sensitive than I realised. I look at her wrist. Her arm jangles with wooden bangles but there's no tattoo that I can see. All the same, she may have a gift for discernment, while Redwood is blind to what's happening in front of his eyes.

Aware of what I'm up to, Nana winks at me and gives me her special smile. Then she begins.

'The task we've given you and your sisters, Linet, isn't an easy one. It's particularly difficult for you here because most of the people around us don't appreciate the old ways as they once did. Cornwall's better than some places, I suppose. We're still close to the land and sea, but just about everywhere else...' Nana shakes her head and downs some more fizz.

Nervous, unsure of what to say next, she glances at her friends. They nod, urging her on.

'I appreciate that what I've created for us here, a life way out on the moor by the lake, takes some getting used to. If I were to do it all over again, maybe I'd raise you differently. Perhaps I wouldn't tie you up in knots of secrecy or bind you to silence. But when the people around us no longer believe in the old ways, it's best to remain silent. That's what my mother and grandmother taught me, and their mothers before them. What happened to Old Hester all those years ago is part and parcel of who we Merrimores are today, so I'm not sure what else I could have done.'

Rosie and Redwood agree, then Redwood adds: 'You did your level best, Zelda. No doubt about it.'

Nana clears her throat. 'It's different for Zula and Adoma,' she says. 'They live in places where some folk remember the old ways, and still feel connected. But if you ask your sisters, they'll tell you that even so, people in their parts of the world are sometimes murdered for what we do, murdered for simply practising our craft.'

'Nana, what are you trying to tell me?'

She glances again at her friends, a furtive gleam in her eyes. Another slug of fizz slips down her gullet.

That's another thing that's puzzling me. Nana doesn't usually drink this quickly. I smell trepidation rising from her skin: a smoky, brackish scent like the lake before a thunderstorm. My sisters sense it too.

'What's going on, Linet?' Zula hisses.

'I don't know,' I reply.

To which Adoma whispers: 'At least she's not talking in proverbs. It's like picking lice out of rice when Gran-pa unleashes proverbs on me. I never understand what he's saying.'

I straighten my shoulders, flip back my hair and concentrate: 'Go on, Nana...'

'What I'm trying to tell you, is that even though I've raised you to think otherwise, we're not, in fact, alone. There are quite a few of us, not enough of course: men and women, mostly women, followers of the craft. We organise in secret. You and your sisters are part of a larger network. I want you to know that...'

'Nana, look at me.' She lifts her downcast eyes and turns her head towards mine. When my eyes lock with hers, I say calmly and clearly: 'Nana, I don't care about those other people. I want to know what's going to happen to *us*: you and me, Zula and her father, Adoma and her gran-pa. Tell me what you've seen!'

She downs the last of her fizz and gets up to replenish her drink as well as those of her friends.

I smell that scent again of a storm closing in on the lake as dark clouds roll in and hover overhead. I finger my talisman, close my eyes, and clear as a smudge of ink on blotting paper, an image surfaces: Nana in a white cotton robe walking to the lake. My eyes snap open. I shake my head. Did I just see what I thought I saw?

My breath quickens and Adoma responds: 'What is it?'

'Did you see something?' asks Zula.

I nod, rubbing my eyelids to erase the blot. 'I thought I saw my grandmother... but it can't be...'

They take my word for it.

I watch Nana pottering about in the kitchen. Watch her crush more ice. Pour sloe gin, open another bottle of pop.

Once she's sitting down again, she gulps half of her drink before saying: 'What I'm trying to tell you, is that once a circle is broken, it has ripple effects in other parts of the world. In the same way that what those miners are doing in Ghana and Mongolia will eventually affect us here, now that Zula's grandma is gone, her death has repercussions on those of us she left behind: Zula's father, Okomfo Gran-pa and me.'

'Ain't that the truth,' Redwood says stroking his chin. 'Once a link's broken, the centre cannot hold.'

Rosie agrees with him and Nana replies: 'The law of cause and effect.'

I must look mystified, for my grandmother sighs: 'What I'm trying to explain to you, Linet dear, is that you're really not alone. Rosie and Redwood here have agreed to keep an eye on you should anything happen to me. I'm not saying it will, mind you – but if something does occur, you should get in touch with them immediately.'

I open my mouth, aghast: 'They'll make me live with my mother, won't they? A mother I don't know, the woman who tried to drown me.'

More silence. Only this time, after another exchange of glances, there's a glint of horror in the eyes of her friends while a blush rises on Nana's face.

'You've misunderstood me. If anything happens to *me*, I've asked Rosie and Redwood to be your legal guardians.'

'But I don't know them either! Surely it can't be as bad you think. What have you seen, Nana? Tell me the truth.'

'I wish I had the words, but I don't. I've got a feeling that whatever's coming our way will be here soon. And from what I've been able to glean from the Tarot cards, it's going to knock the stuffing right out of me, and leave us dazed, running around like headless chickens. Forgive me, but that's all I can say.'

16
Adoma

My friend, it took a while to find a way through the haze sprinkled on us by Nana Merrimore's words. Just like Gran-pa and his old man proverbs, she had us spinning, not knowing in which direction to turn: north, south, east or west? Or should we dig a hiding place for ourselves deep in the earth instead? Believe me when I tell you that listening to her that day was like trying to see through a dust storm.

Imagine everything covered in grime inside and out. And beyond, as far as the eye can see, a blur of shapes grainy with sand from the Sahara wind we call the harmattan. When it blows old people and babies cough, some die and just about everyone ends up sneezing, until, half-blind, we rub our eyes to clear them of grit. During the season of inclement wind, there is grit everywhere.

That's how we felt that night: blinded and distracted by words underlined by fear that we didn't fully understand. Our teacher, distressed, was not herself. What's more, her warnings had an undertow that seemed to drag her from us, while on the shore we tried to call her back.

Our remedy was to talk. We dissected her words. What did she mean by saying we were not alone? Of course we weren't alone! I'd never thought so, and neither had Zula.

It's not that I could say, hand on heart, that I'd seen wrists with tattoos such as ours, but just because I hadn't, meant nothing. Maybe one day we would; then we would know, as surely as one hand cannot clap by itself, that there are others like us. We realised, if the three of us were custodians of sacred sites, there must be hallowed places elsewhere, places with caretakers who cherished them and would be as devastated as we had been when our sanctuary in Ashanti was desecrated.

What surprised us – if what Nana Merrimore said was true – was how organised we were. In fact, one of the first questions we asked ourselves that night was how we could make contact, if we needed to, with others like ourselves?

'Pa will know,' Zula said. 'I'll ask him tomorrow.'

'And I'll ask Okomfo Gran-pa as well,' I decided. 'We need to find out in case anything happens to our teachers. Do you seriously think they're in danger?'

'Your grandma believed so, Zula. And now so does Nana.'

'I was thinking that myself,' Zula confessed, before shuddering and shaking her head.

We were sitting in a circle on Linet's bed.

Linet stroked her talisman: 'Nana's changing. It's as if...' She paused: 'It's as if she wants to foist me on those strangers.'

'Didn't you like them?' asked Zula.

'They seemed a little...'

'Weird?' I suggested.

Linet nodded. 'And here's another thing, I've never heard anyone call Nana *sweetheart* before. Do you think...'

I jumped in: 'Eh-eh, my sister! I beg you on my knees. Do. Not. Go. There.'

'But we're there already,' Zula smiled. 'Your nana and that long thin man? Eeei!'

'I was only wondering,' said Linet. 'You can't fault me for thinking about Nana's past when it's a lot easier than fretting over what she said today.'

Linet moved to the window seat of her bedroom and looking out at the lake, allowed Bracken to jump on to her lap.

Little by little, as she gazed on water, I began to realise it was feeding her, like a mother nurturing a baby in the womb. Having revealed her past, the lake, and its drowning pool, seemed to cradle my sister as if preparing to take Nana Merrimore back. I felt the heft of the cord between the lake and Linet, the throb and flow of emotion as from one moment to the next their pulses coiled, circling each other until they started beating in time.

To see through the haze of Nana Merrimore's words and grasp their meaning, I listened to Gran-pa's voice, the voice I carried within me.

'If your instincts are correct, Adoma,' I heard him say. 'And your instincts often coincide with mine, then it is my humble opinion that Nana Merrimore is preparing to make a journey to her village, a journey from which no one returns.' Returning to the village is an old man's way of talking about death.

My heart reeled. So Zula's grandmother had been right. I inhaled deeply, tiptoeing around the fact that a possibility of an ending might also explain Gran-pa's behaviour recently: cantankerous and reckless, he'd started behaving like a man with nothing to lose.

Before my imagination could dip a toe in a pool of snapping crocodiles, I recoiled. Having swallowed the thought and sealed my lips, I chose to concentrate on Linet's grandmother. What had been unnerving was the drumbeat of fear I'd sensed at her core. But as Gran-pa had once said to me: 'Who knows how each of us will react when danger knocks on our door? Will you smile and let him in, Adoma? Or run and hide? Nobody knows, grandchild. Neither you or I, because the roots of fear run deep and its fruit is poisonous.'

'Okomfo Gran-pa will know how to help,' I said to Linet. 'I'll ask him.'

'I'll find out what I can from Pa as well,' Zula added. 'He'll have an inkling if Nana's shell is cracking like a chick about to be born.'

The hairs on my neck bristled. The cracking of an egg, a chick about to be born, is yet another way of talking about death. Zula and I appreciated this, leeching any hope we still held.

It was well after dusk by now. The light of a full moon shining on the lake's surface illuminated the silhouette of oak trees at its edge. Opening the window, Linet pulled back curtains that framed the room. A profusion of moonbeams flooded in as she turned from the lake, its reflection still playing on her face and hands, still humming in her heart.

'I'm not sure of anything anymore,' she said. 'I can't tell if Nana's lying to protect me, or simply telling the truth. All I know is she's terrified. Are your teachers scared as well?'

'Not that I've noticed,' said Zula. 'Pa's grieving, but that hasn't stopped him talking to our friends and neighbours. We've made a decision to challenge the company prospecting for copper and coal in the mountains. We don't want the Sleeping Giant touched. Who but a fool would destroy the source of water that we use for ourselves and our livestock?'

'Then *we* must be fools,' I concluded. 'I've heard people saying that poisoning our river with cyanide and mercury will be worth it if they find gold.' I squeezed my mouth, kissing my lips. 'Money talks big time everywhere. Okomfo Gran-pa's the only person I know who isn't greedy for it. If anything, he's taking more risks than ever now.'

'How?' asked Zula.

'He's as angry as a soldier ant at those *galamsey* people and yet he blames the chief for what's happening. When he goes to see him, he threatens to take the whole lot of them to court.'

Zula nodded: 'Pa and his friends have sent a delegation to speak to our government. We're not expecting much, but Pa says the very least we should do is try...'

'We all have to try harder,' said Linet. 'Try harder and do things differently...'

'Perhaps we should use more magic,' I suggested. 'If Gran-pa hadn't stopped me, I'd have blasted the chief when I met him. And as for those miners, I'd have flung them in the air.' I sighed, unable to hide my frustration. 'Gran-pa says it's better to take them to court because the law's on our side.'

'But the law's slow,' Zula replied. 'In any case, Grandma said people high up don't listen to the likes of us.'

'*Poor on earth*,' I sniffed, '*a loser everywhere!*'

Linet pulled a nightdress over her head and sat on the bed, completing our circle. 'What I'd like to know is, should we keep doing what our teachers have done, if it's not working anymore?'

Her words settled like a stone lobbed into a pond, its ripples scudding out as Zula chucked another in: 'Perhaps we should be more open about how we protect our shrines.'

'You mean use magic *openly*?' I shook my head. 'Gran-pa's right to be cautious. Nothing would please me more than to blast those miners to pieces. But we took an oath to protect life. What comes naturally to us is scary to outsiders.' I clicked my fingers. 'They'd kill us just like that if they saw us use magic.'

'That doesn't mean we shouldn't change tack,' Zula replied. 'Our teachers are *Sankofa*. They returned to their roots to teach us what they know. They've helped us grow into *nsoromma*. Maybe when our time comes, we'll find another way to protect our sites.'

A possibility seized me. 'What about a squad of sky-warriors?' I clapped my hands. 'With the right contacts, we can connect, pool our gifts and use them to defend our sanctuaries.'

'We'll be different,' Linet added, her face still flushed from the lake. 'We'll find a way to replenish your river, Adoma. We can't make the trees grow back quickly, but once we've forced those miners out, we can clean the river, help it flow again and plant more trees.'

'We should do it!' I cried.

The lock on her forehead gleaming moonstone bright, Zula took Linet and I by the hand. 'Listen carefully. Before Grandma died she said to me: "*Tell your sisters, unless the three of you use every morsel of what's inside you, we shall never defeat today's skin-walkers.*"'

A wolfish shine entered Zula's eyes. Ears pricked, her gaze fixed, I felt a sensation of ice creep over my skin as her excitement gripped me.

'All those years ago, when we first met at the Giant's mouth,' she went on, 'I sensed others with us: creatures and birds that open us up to greater insights. Have you noticed any changes in you recently?'

I remembered the image of a leopard flashing through my mind as the river goddess' shrine was destroyed. And, the last time we'd met at the Giant's mouth, I recalled that when I placed my brow against Zula's, I'd felt the leap of a leopard in my heart; not to mention the strange sensations I now experienced during my night travels. Eager to understand, I answered, 'Yes...'

While Linet, rubbing her chest, replied: 'There's a bird in me. Only today on the moor, when I needed a cloak of feathers to keep out the wind, I called on it.'

'I saw the cloak,' I confirmed.

I placed Linet's fingers against my cheek, relieved we were talking about a transformation we'd both sensed but hadn't been able to put into words. The more I thought about it, the greater a recollection of animal warmth surfaced: a shadowy creature with paws that clawed the bark of trees whenever I set foot in the forest.

'Mine's definitely a leopard,' I admitted. 'Sometimes it slides between my legs as if it wants to trip me over. It craves my attention.'

'Of course it does! Our spirit creatures are a part of us, our special gift. I am wolf.' Her grey eyes sparking yellow as her spirit shone through, Zula smiled. 'Come, my sisters.'

17
Adoma

✳

I woke up, pulse racing, Zula's revelation buzzing in my ears, eyes, heart, my everything. Acknowledging our spirit creatures was all very well but displaying them could be lethal.

For an instant my senses grappled with what I'd experienced that night. Before I could take stock and delve deeper, I sniffed, suspicious of a change in the atmosphere. The hair in my ears bristled, identifying a strange jarring vibration. I sniffed again and as my nostrils inhaled the cloying scent of incense, my heart hammered faster than a starving man pounding fufu. *Boom! Boom!* The mother of all dangers was upon me! A menace I was familiar with had entered Granpa's house!

Anyone watching would think as I sprang off my sleeping mat that the mat and my cover cloth were on fire. Yet there was no smoke to be seen and no fire to speak of. What convinced me was the smell wafting through the house.

It seeped beneath the doors: the door to the corridor and the one that opened into my grandparents' bedroom. It meant one thing alone. My mother was home. Whenever she returned to visit us, Sweet Mother, as she insisted I call her, burned incense to rid the house of spirits: evil spirits.

I tied my sleeping cloth around me and ran into the courtyard. I ran to embrace the only creature I knew, apart from Gran-pa, who understood what it was like to be separated from a mother at a tender age. Standing at the bottom of a wizened, old neem tree, I yelled: 'Milo! Milo! Are you there?'

Milo showed his face and then hid behind one of the tree's towering boughs. He didn't enjoy my mother's visits any more than I did.

'Come down, Milo,' I pleaded.

He peeped out again and with a glum expression on his face, shook his head.

'Coward! You want me to face her alone?'

Gnashing his teeth, Milo produced the screeching noises he makes when he's scared and wants to terrify those who would prey on him. He had every reason to be wary of my mother. On a previous visit, she'd dared Gran-ma to cook her favourite bush stew, insinuating that what she hankered for most in the world was monkey meat. To make matters worse, to rub pepper in the wound of Milo's hurt pride and my open-mouthed horror, she found the incident so entertaining she couldn't stop laughing at us for days.

'OK,' I said to Milo. 'Stay up there if you have to, but the least you can do is come down and greet me.'

As stubborn as a child who's never had to fill his belly with water to help him sleep, but has been raised to eat jolloff rice his whole life, Milo hissed at me and shook his head.

'Let's hope her visit isn't long, otherwise...'

'I take it you're talking about your mother.' Gran-pa, already dressed for the day, placed a hand on my shoulder. I turned to face him and, linking his fingers in mine, smiled.

His hands were gnarled and rough – the hands of a man who works on the land nurturing seedlings and plants, a man who cultivates food to eat: yam, cassava, plantain and bananas. My grandparents and I grew most of the food we ate and yet Gran-pa still made time to see clients who came to him for healing and advice.

I nodded. Yes, I had been talking to Milo about my mother. 'Why's she come to visit us this time?'

'Your grandmother wants her to talk sense into me.'

'Gran-ma's worried,' I said. 'And so am I, Gran-pa.'

'Well you shouldn't be. I haven't believed – all these years – in what I do, what I'm about, to back down now.'

'But Gran-pa...' I wanted to let him know that I understood his resolute stand was about more than belief and principle. He was hurt, deeply hurt by the behaviour of our fellow citizens and their foreign partners. So was I.

I continued holding his hand until, unable to find words that said what I wanted to say, Gran-pa hushed my stuttering. He told me to hurry up and take my morning bath because on that day, a Saturday, he wanted me to accompany him on yet another of his visits to the chief's palace.

'I need you to be with me as a witness, Adoma,' he said, 'in case the unexpected happens.'

'What do you mean by "unexpected", Gran-pa?'

He wouldn't say. He simply shook his head before stating that he planned to leave for the palace as soon as I'd welcomed my mother home and made breakfast for her.

I quickly fetched water and bathed. I pulled on a pair of jeans and t-shirt and, eager to jump the hurdle of my mother's homecoming and land safely on the other side, I filled a pail with water from our well for my mother to use. It was then, and only then, that I knocked on the door of my grandparents' bedroom.

No response.

I knocked a second time and detected movement on the other side.

I was about to knock again when the door swung open. Vapours of incense enveloped me as through a thick haze of grey, my mother emerged.

I've been told that I resemble her. She is almost as tall as Gran-pa. Athletic in build, she has a striking ebony face graced with almond-shaped eyes. Her hair, bundled in a hairnet, is long and jet-black, while mine, cropped short, has a dark reddish tinge to it.

'Adoma, come in,' she said smiling. 'Let me pray for you, child.'

I remained at the doorway. 'I've fetched water for your bath. I'm making your breakfast right now.'

She beckoned me closer: 'Come,' she insisted, offering her hand. 'I've got a present for you.'

I took a step back. 'Breakfast now, prayers later?' I turned and ran down the corridor shouting: 'Welcome home, Sweet Mother!'

Back in our outdoor kitchen, I stirred cornmeal dough and liquid in a bowl and then adding it bit by bit to a pan of boiling water, made porridge on a charcoal fire. I covered the pot to keep it warm, then cut and buttered two slices of bread in which I inserted a hastily fried egg. And all the time as I cooked and laid a breakfast tray for my mother, while I placed a large side table in front of Old Freedom and put a spoon on it, I allowed myself to hurl silent abuse at the woman I called Sweet Mother after her favourite hi-life song – a song she used to play again and again on Gran-pa's radio cassette player.

I shook a broom in her face, cackling at the prospect that although I was not quite as tall as she was, I soon would be. And when the moment came and I was able to glare at her, eyeball to eyeball, I promised myself that I would tell her exactly what I thought of the prayers she bombarded me with; prayers she believed would save my soul even though I helped Gran-pa at our shrines – the one that used to be in the forest, the other at the back of our yard.

Simmering with rage, I allowed ancient memories to fan my frustration. For example: after she left me with my grandparents to forge a new life for herself, my mother married the leader of the Church of Spiritual Redemption, Pastor Elisha, and was admitted into his church and embraced it whole-heartedly.

With her new faith came problems I sensed long ago, when I was small as a chick scampering in Gran-pa's yard. Time after time through insinuation and sneers, I noticed my mother's contempt for what Nana Merrimore calls the Old Ways. Gran-pa, Sweet Mother declared, perhaps with Gran-ma at his side, was certain to writhe in the flames of hell for eternity.

Imagine someone telling you that as a child! And when that someone is your own mother... I bit my lip to taste the memory again. With it came a stab of irritation as I remembered what I'd done after she explained the difference between heaven and hell to me. I'd crawled beneath Old Freedom and, rolling in dust, wept tears of fury.

Sweet Mother? Once I started thinking about her, there was no end to it. It was like scratching a scab that never comes off, rubbing a sore that cannot heal.

I was still picking at it when I knocked again on my grandparents' door. 'Sweet Mother, your food is ready,' I said.

'Coming,' she replied.

A few minutes later she strolled into the sitting room wearing a vibrant yellow *bou-bou*, a long, flowing robe that flattered her figure. On her hair was a matching head wrap that flapped up and down the way a frightened cockerel does when it's determined to fly. By the time Sweet Mother had bustled over to Old Freedom and planted her behind on it, I was ready with a pot of hot water for her tea. She poured herself a cup and started eating.

Before she was halfway through the porridge, I was fidgeting, itching to be on the road with Granpa. I tried to exercise patience by counting to myself. When that didn't work, I decided to place a bet. I bet you, Adoma, I told myself, before you reach thirty Sweet Mother will have told you off.

I began counting, but as I did so, I wriggled and twisting my fingers behind my back, rose up and down on my heels as if an ant had found its way into my pants.

Sweet Mother glanced in my direction and I savoured a gleam of disappointment in her black coral eyes: 'Adoma, what is the matter with you?'

'Gran-pa told me to hurry,' I confessed. 'He's asked me to accompany him to the chief's palace.'

'Is he involving you in his nonsense as well? I forbid it!'

There it was – the first lash of disapproval and I hadn't got up to twenty! I struggled not to smile.

'You think I'm joking do you? Then think again! You are not going anywhere with your grandfather.' My mother pushed her empty bowl of porridge to one side and took a savage bite of egg sandwich.

I waited until her mouth was full, waited until she was chomping heartily, before I raised the question I'd been asking my age-mates at school to rally support for our cause: mine and Gran-pa's: 'Don't you care when trees are cut down in the forest and cyanide and mercury are used in a sacred river to mine gold? Don't you care that most of the river's fish are dead or not fit to eat? And that now it's poisoned, no one upstream can use its water: not for drinking, washing or farming.'

Sweet Mother sighed. 'Of course I care, Adoma!'

'You don't care enough. If you did you'd help Gran-pa and me do something about it.'

Sweet Mother shook her head. 'This is Ghana,

Adoma, and your grandfather is going about this business the wrong way...'

Before I could answer back, Gran-ma, behind me, interrupted: 'And what would you say is the right way, daughter?'

'Indeed,' chuckled Gran-pa. 'Tell me what I'm doing wrong and I'll heed your advice. I may be old, but I'm willing to learn new tricks if it'll help our cause.'

'In that case, Pa, sit down and listen.'

18

Adoma

※ ※

'Pa,' Sweet Mother said, when he and Gran-ma were sitting opposite her on stools, 'this is Ghana and you know as well as anyone, that you shouldn't harass a chief backed by big politicians and businessmen.'

'Are you saying, my daughter, that the rule of law no longer applies to every citizen of our land? Are you telling me, your father, that we should no longer follow our ancestors and husband our resources and use them well?'

'Anyone would think to hear you talk that our ancestors were perfect. They were not!' Sweet Mother cried.

Gran-pa covered his weathered face with a hand and sighed. Gran-ma, her eyes downcast, straightened the faded cloth she was wearing and glanced at my mother. The more father and daughter argued, the

more eloquently Gran-ma's eyes spoke of her devotion
to Gran-pa and her alarm at the trail he was following.

'Listen, Pa,' said my mother. 'Have you given any
thought to what Ma and Adoma will do, if, God
forbid, the worst happens to you?'

My fingertips tingled at the boldness of my mother's
tongue, its ability to probe and hurt anyone who
crossed her, even my grandfather. And when Gran-pa
winced, I was minded to spring to his defence, to
channel energy from the earth and sky through my
fingers, bind it to the fury coiled within me and then
release it in a seamless blast from my mind. I was
sorely tempted to strike Sweet Mother down, but
with Gran-pa's lessons weighing on my conscience,
his reminders not to use my talent in anger but to be
strategic and tactical in all that I did, I refrained.

Even though my fingers twitched, hungry to
act, and I flexed my wrists in readiness, I held back
while Gran-pa looked down at a pair of worn leather
sandals that had been mended many times. Every day,
without fail, he polished them to a shine because his
sandals were faithful friends who did what they were
meant to do: they kept dust off his feet.

Once she had started, Sweet Mother wouldn't let
go. She was wild, I tell you, her teeth sinking through
hide and flesh, to the jugular. And like the wildcat
she was, she assailed Okomfo Gran-pa from every
direction: it wasn't just Gran-ma and me he should

think of, she said. What about those clients who depended on him for counsel and advice? Not to mention her family in Accra, her children with Pastor Elisha, who she had named after Esther the Beautiful Queen and God's most favoured one, King David.

'And here's another thing,' Sweet Mother said. 'I have it on the highest authority from a member of our church, that no good will come from pointing fingers at what they're doing. Pa, you know they have the backing of everyone necessary, so stop it! Stop what you're doing.'

Sweet Mother readjusted her buttocks and with a finger wagging in the air, was leaning forwards when Gran-ma interrupted: 'Daughter, I asked you here to *talk* to your father, not to scold him like a small boy.'

Eyes shut tight, Sweet Mother squeezed her face, then with a finger on her lips refrained from talking until, having drained poison from her tongue, she said: 'Pa, I apologise. I don't mean to disrespect you, but before you continue your crusade against bribery and corruption, let me remind you of the country we live in. This be Ghana-oh! And everyone from the Big Man up top to the smallest pickney down below, we all dey chop-chop.'

Gran-pa snorted in disgust: 'Does your husband chop-chop?' he asked. 'Do you take bribes, my daughter? Does he? Because even if you and your husband choose to follow the crowd, I do not.'

'Have mercy, Pa!' Sweet Mother wailed. 'Why are you so stubborn?'

Gran-pa smiled as Gran-ma brushed away a tear. She moved quickly but not before Gran-pa had seen it. He placed a large hand over her smaller one and embraced it in a gesture of affection I'd witnessed only once before. On the day they'd celebrated their fortieth year of marriage, he'd proclaimed to the assembled guests that if he were to live his life again, he'd choose Gran-ma for his wife a second time. And if, after he died, he found himself back on earth, he would travel the highways and byways of the world until he found Gran-ma and married her once again.

That morning my chest tightened as I watched them.

And when Gran-ma looked up at Gran-pa and said: 'Husband, I know it's not easy for you but please, for all our sakes, listen to our daughter,' Gran-pa raised her hand to his cheek and kissed it.

My friend, believe me when I tell you that in this my country, Ghana, we do not do what they do in Linet's land. We do not kiss-kiss and touchy-feel every minute of the day. Apart from a few people who walk around hand in hand, just about everything else takes place in darkness. So believe me when I say that I have never, my whole life long, seen Okomfo Gran-pa kiss any part of Gran-ma's body. Never! And yet I witnessed it that morning with my own eyes *filii filii*!

My mouth opened. My jaw dropped and my heart swelled, convinced that if my One and Only and I could be as true and kind to each other as they were, if we could follow the path laid by Gran-pa and Gran-ma, maybe one-day, one-day, Kofi Agyeman and I would be fortunate enough to taste their happiness.

Gran-pa nodded and listened, his eyes half-closed like an old lizard basking in the sun, while he attended to what Gran-ma was saying: 'I asked our daughter to talk to you today because I have never, in all our time together, husband, seen you behave in this manner. Our chief, who was once our friend, is now your enemy. Our neighbours no longer go out of their way to talk to me. Why? On the chief's orders!'

'You see!' Sweet Mother cried, standing up. 'You see, Pa!' she said bounding towards him with the speed of a tigress about to pounce. 'This is all *your* doing. Leave this nonsense behind you! Walk away from it. If not for me, for Ma and Adoma's sake at least!'

My mother had a point. Her fervour prompted Gran-pa's question about what each of us would do should danger knock on our door to clamour in my mind. And in my heart I felt a fierce scratching, a snarl of alarm as I recognised that this was Gran-pa's moment, his future in the balance.

He lifted his eyes to the ceiling as if begging a superior being for assistance in withstanding Sweet Mother's attack: 'Am I to blame,' he asked, his gimlet gaze piercing hers, 'if our chief behaves foolishly and rattles like groundnut shells in a broken calabash? Is it my fault if our countrymen upriver have to buy water to drink now? *My* fault that our fishermen no longer find fish to feed their families?'

Their fingers still entwined, Gran-ma laid Gran-pa's hand against *her* cheek. My mouth opened again.

'You are not to blame,' said Gran-ma. 'Nevertheless, I'm begging you, husband, do not make me a widow while our bones are yet strong. Do not make me grieve while we can still relish this life of ours. Husband, do not leave me to gaze in my pot of pebbles alone, for what I have seen in it does not bode well.'

Gran-ma's words snuffed the last flickers of anger from the conversation but as her premonition fluttered like a moth in a corner of the room, I held my breath. We all did because in our different ways we each of us felt the shiver of the moth's wings flitting closer.

Gran-pa sighed. Then with his eyes dancing with hers, he replied: 'Wife, would you have me behave in a way that I cannot? Would you have me be other than what I am?'

Gran-ma shook her head. Between one moment and the next, the tilt from one side to the other, her face quivered and time froze. In that second I glimpsed Gran-pa's fate and trembled. Danger was at his door and he was opening it.

'And you, Adoma?' Gran-pa asked. 'Would you have me behave otherwise?'

For a moment I was tempted to side with Sweet Mother and force him to change course. Avoiding the delve of his eyes, the deep dive of them that exposed my soul to his, I looked at my feet, praying that Kwame, the creator of all creatures in this world and the next, would do everything in his power to prevent Gran-pa venturing outside and thereby keep us safe. In that instant I was almost persuaded to lie. But I could not. Even after what I'd glimpsed, after Nana Merrimore's voice came back to me and I heard her say: '*Whatever's coming our way will be here soon,*' what else was there for me to do but to stand firm as tendrils of fear slithered around my ankles, binding me to the floor?

I shook myself, stamped on my terror and met Gran-pa's gaze: 'I'm with you Gran-pa,' I said. 'I'm with you all the way.'

As the words left my lips, Sweet Mother hissed.

🐾

Gran-pa and I would have reached the chief's palace within the hour if my One and Only hadn't met us at the gate of our compound. Kofi was with his mother. Felicia, known as Auntie Feli, the sole provider for her family, a market woman cursed with a cauldron of ailments that needed constant attention – which she received at a cheaper price from Gran-pa than from a medical doctor. If it wasn't the wheeziness in her chest, her stomach would be hurting her. And if not her stomach, it was rheumatism in her joints or excruciating pain in her legs, the result of long hours on her feet at the market.

At the sight of her the fear creeping through my veins eased somewhat. Kwame, the creator of all creatures great and small, was smiling on us at last! Because with Auntie Feli at our house, there was no chance of us leaving the compound before nightfall.

She hauled Kofi into our yard by the neck, pushed him down the path past the neem tree to a grove of fruiting lemon, orange and guava trees overshadowed by a huge mango. Beneath its branches, Auntie Feli shoved her son on to a stool.

'Okomfo!' she cried. 'Help me! Help my son. Cast out this nonsense of football that's taken hold of his mind. Make it so he can study with a clear mind and pass his exams! Okomfo! Help us!'

Kofi glanced at me making it clear that if I so much as tittered, if I so much as remarked on the events I was about to see, I would score an own goal and lose his friendship. The smile on my lips shrivelled.

'Feli, bring your boy another time,' said Gran-pa. 'You've caught us on our way out.'

Another time? Auntie Feli had no intention of

leaving and barrelled on: 'Okomfo, someone has cursed us with football madness because this boy of mine thinks and dreams about one thing alone. Football! His dreams are wild, I tell you. So wild he wants to travel to *abrokyire* on a football scholarship. If he's not playing with your girl-child over there, he's practising with his team. Make him stop, Okomfo. Make him drink one of your concoctions to purge him of this illness. And then make him sit down and study. Okomfo, I beg you!'

Arms outstretched, Aunt Feli fell onto her knees. She flinched. I shook my head. Rheumatism.

'Please, Okomfo, please!' she grovelled.

I helped her back to her feet and into a chair beside Kofi's stool. When she was safely ensconced I slipped behind the guava tree and, hugging my ribs, heaved with silent laughter. The pungent scent of ripening fruit tickled my nostrils, while I listened, squatting beneath the tree.

'He never studies,' Auntie Feli said of Kofi. 'Kotoko! Chelsea! Everything's Kotoko or Chelsea! He used to talk about Michael Essien morning, noon and night. Now, every day: Pogba! Pogba! Pogba!'

A hand on her hip, she swung around to glare at my One and Only as if she was on the verge of throttling him.

'Okomfo, what am I to do when this my eldest, the only one of my three with the brains to elevate us, won't do what he's told and concentrate on chewing his books?'

Having already thanked Kwame for delaying our departure, I urged him to cancel our outing completely.

'Please,' I said to him, 'make Auntie Feli talk so much about her problem with my One and Only that before we know it the morning is over and we have to visit the chief another day.'

'Feli,' said Gran-pa, 'what you believe to be a curse may be a blessing in disguise. Does your boy respect you?'

Kofi's mother grunted.

'Does he steal?'

'No, Okomfo.'

'So your problem is that he doesn't work hard enough?'

She grunted again.

'Kofi, are you willing to change your habits and spend more time with your books?'

Gran-pa's question was met with silence.

I turned as my grandfather repeated it. Kofi's face was as dark as an afternoon sky in the rainy season, the first drops about to fall. My heart heaved, almost capsizing as I felt the weight of his humiliation followed by a twinge of tenderness so intense it hurt. I tell you, my friend, we Asante are a proud people, none more so than a boy raised by a woman on her own; a woman who lives in the hope that her eldest, a boy, will excel.

I got up from the ground and, crouching by Kofi, whispered his name: 'Okomfo Gran-pa's talking to you. Answer him.' I nudged him by linking my little finger with his and felt him shiver, felt his tears slide down his cheeks as if I was crying myself. Kofi placed a hand over his face and half-sobbing, waited until, able to speak once again, he told his version of the football story. And all the while, as Gran-pa, Auntie Feli and I listened, a sun lark in the guava tree, having satisfied her hunger, lit up the sky with a bright new song.

19

Adoma

✳

'You like him,' Gran-pa said after Kofi and his mother had left, each content with the truce the old man had brokered: Kofi promised to play football only at the weekend, the rest of the time he would spend on his books.

'He's my one, true friend,' I replied. 'My one and only.'

'The one and only?'

I nodded. 'One of these days I intend to be like this with him, Gran-pa.' I folded my middle finger over my forefinger, touching them to my cheek as my face glowed. 'When the time comes, I hope I'll treat him with the same respect and loving-kindness you show Gran-ma.'

'He's not frightened by what you do for the river goddess?'

I shook my head. 'At times I think he'd like to use her to win at football, but I know better, Gran-pa.'

'Good girl.' A smile rippled over my grandfather's features, lighting his eyes.

Head tilted, I paused. And gauging the warp and weft of him, the texture of his weave, I found myself nestling at the source of his being and remembered. Not so long ago, I used to sit on Gran-pa's knee while I stroked the dent on his forehead. A friend had injured him when they were children. 'He took a stone,' Gran-pa had said. 'And hit me right here.'

I recalled his forefinger guiding mine as I explored the dent and then the rest of his face: stubborn bristles of hair on chin and jaw, lips that hid a tongue that never belittled but encouraged me to conserve what our ancestors had left in our care. Gran-pa was the kindest, most fearless man I knew, and I loved him more than anyone else, loved him even more than Milo and Kofi. I needed him by my side a while longer.

So, instead of making light of my separation from most of my age group as I usually did, this time I chose to dwell on it: 'You've taught me to rely on my sisters,' I reminded him. 'Because to belong to the shrine is not a popular choice.'

'How so?' Gran-pa asked.

This was his way of teaching me to flex the muscles of my mind to better understand my calling. He would ask the same question again and again to help me walk firmly on the path I was on.

'Because Gran-pa, those Alleluia worshippers in my class worry me too much.'

Gran-pa nodded.

'You know how it is, Gran-pa. They make the same *wahala* Sweet Mother does. They never stop telling me that what we do is worship trees and rivers. While they claim to worship their one true god, their three in one, they say we spill the blood of animals, sacrifice babies, practise *ju-ju*...'

'And how do you answer them, Adoma?'

I inhaled the scent of Gran-pa's skin like I used to when I was small enough to sit on his lap. I held the smell of him, savouring a trace of wood smoke and sprinklings of nutmeg that Gran-ma used in stews and cakes. The scent enfolded me.

'I tell them what you told me long ago, Gran-pa,' I replied. 'Our god being such a bountiful god wouldn't have stopped at having just *one* son. He has many sons. Daughters as well...'

Gran-pa laughed. 'Spoken like a true Ashanti!'

By now, despite my best efforts to delay our departure – my attempt to persuade Milo down from the neem tree, followed by a last minute suggestion that for his audience with the chief Gran-pa should change into a kente cloth – a colourful, woven cloth worn on important occasions – we were heading out of the gate once again. I carried a rucksack containing water while Gran-pa, behind me, steered his scooter.

As I pulled back the lock to let him through, he gazed at me and said: 'You've seen my fate, haven't you, grandchild? You've seen. That's why I know you're ready for me to go...'

'Gran-pa...'

We were in the din and bustle of our street among vendors selling their wares. A Hausa man cycled past us, a pile of material strapped on his bicycle. Opposite, a woman, a straw hat shielding her face from the sun, roasted corn on a wood fire. Beside her a child wrapped portions of plantain and groundnuts.

I said his name and Gran-pa smiled. At that moment a motorbike thundered down the lane. Two macho men in helmets, biceps pumped to bursting, sped towards us. A second before they passed, the larger of the two on the passenger seat, raised his hand. In it was a gun, which he levelled at Gran-pa. The clap of a firecracker exploded in my ears. One second and Gran-pa's smile snapped into open-mouthed surprise. He looked down at his hand, wet with blood, as if it belonged to a stranger, the wound in his stomach to someone else.

'Gran-pa!' I shouted. I turned, and before the motorbike could exceed my range, made a fist of my mind, and summoning the powers of earth and sky, wind and fire, hurled arrows of molten rage at the assailants.

The motorbike skidded.

In me a volcano erupted and a leopard roared.

No one hurts Okomfo Gran-pa while I'm around. And when I'm riled, no skin-walker escapes my grasp.

I unleashed a volley of blasts that pummelled the hitman and his driver on their shoulders, arms and legs.

Brakes screeched, necks jerked back and the bike flew into the air. For an instant the driver clung on, before he and the hitman tumbled to the ground, and the motorbike dropped on them. The crash ignited screams of pain, frantic juddering of helmets on the ground. The assassin's fingers twitched. His body quivered, then lay still.

I pivoted, springing to Gran-pa's aid. Slumped against the scooter, his eyes were closed. I touched his neck searching for a pulse. But as I did and Gran-ma and Sweet Mother rushed outside to see what the *wahala* was about, I understood that Gran-pa was on his last journey home to his village.

20

Zula

On the day when, one after the other, another of our teachers left us, the sun climbing the sky in Ghana had not reached its zenith. After Grandma's death, Okomfo Gran-pa was next to go. As he began his journey home to his village, Linet, jolted by the memory of ink on a patch of pink, turned to her upstairs window.

I was halfway through watering our livestock in wolf-light. Overhead, a hawk drifting in the sky arched a wing, and blocking the last of the sun, cast her shadow on me. The shadow hovered. I looked up and at that moment a flash of insight set my wolf eyes blazing. I watched events unfold.

On Bodmin Moor I saw what Linet was seeing: Nana Merrimore, head high, back straight, long strides taking her to the lake.

'Nana. Nana, stop,' I hear Linet cry.

Heartbeats drumming, I follow her down the stairs.

'Run, Linet, run,' I tell her.

'Nana! Nana,' she screams. 'Stop!'

She tries to sprint, but Bracken, a cat bewitched, pounces and, clawing at her feet, foils Linet's attempts to run unhindered.

Wolf eyes sharp as a sabre, I race past Linet. In a white nightdress, hair braided, Nana Merrimore sees my shade at the edge of her vision and ignores me.

'Think again,' I tell her sensing her intention. 'Think of Linet!'

Her reply is to open her arms wide and wade into the lake.

'No! No!' Linet sobs.

Deaf to her cries, Nana Merrimore ventures deeper. Dipping, slipping, she croons to the women of the lake as to long-lost sisters and summons them to her side:

'Sister swan, sister auk,
Sister starling, sister hawk.
Sisters of day, sisters of night
Owl, raven, curlew and kite
Watch over my Linet-girl!

But you, sister chough, settle on her,
Red in beak and feet, build a nest for her.

Hold her through life's brawl and squall.
Watch over my Linet-girl, sisters all!'

Nana Merrimore sings as the lake splashes her waist, her chest, her neck. Then with only her head above water, she closes her eyes and with a sigh allows the drowning pool to claim her.

I looked on, stunned, Linet's whimpers of pain in my ears: 'Hush, Linet, hush,' I said to her.

The answer I received was a deafening roar that shook my body. An explosion. Not where I stood by the lake with the hawk overhead but far away. Around me, our camels continued lapping water; our horses continued grazing. Altan, no longer thirsty, was rootling through scrubland for blades of fresh grass when Pa's horse, Takhi, neighed. Altan did the same. Then Takhi, tossing his head, cantered in the direction of where his master was, towards the mountains of the Sleeping Giant.

Ears pricked, Altan sought me out with his muzzle. He brushed against my arm and straight away the scene thrust before me shimmered into motion.

'Pa,' I whispered.

He had left early that morning for the Sleeping Giant in a truck with several herdsmen. According to our sources, in preparation for the mining of copper to begin, an Australian company would start blasting the terrain that day. With our pleas ignored by our government, the plan Pa and his friends conceived, was to make it impossible to damage any part of our sacred space by demonstrating on it. Not a crevice or a canyon of the mountain range would be harmed by skin-walkers. Not when our lives depended on water that after settling in the Giant's mouth ran down into the steppes.

While some of our herdsmen argued with skin-walkers, Pa led two men up a ravine to the site of the proposed blast. The men down below pointed at them. That's when the white men, arms waving, shouted. One of them took out a phone, tapped the keypad and shook his head at the same time as Pa's intuition made him stop and turn. Pa saw arms signalling and alerted his friends. Between them they deciphered the gestures and bolted.

A minute later, the blast sounded, and the mountain shuddered. Columns cracked, shattering into rocks that careened in a tempest of boulders. Blocks tumbled down a side of the Giant and, collapsing into rubble, took on the shape of a crouching Siberian tiger. The tiger growled and for a second, I believed the worst was over. The rocks seemed to slow to a crawl, faltering in their descent before the tiger roared, pelting the valley with pebbles and stones.

I watched, petrified, a prisoner captured in the haze of my grey, unblinking gaze, as Pa, leading his friends, skidded down the mountainside. I tried to call out but couldn't. Tried to point out a path to safety though none existed.

Twisting and turning this way and that, diving to one side, then the other, Pa and his men scrambled for their lives till the moment came when the tiger leaped and, opening its jaws, devoured them in the crush.

I sank to my knees, dazed.

'Pa, Pa,' I kept saying, unable to believe what my eyes had seen or conceive of a world without him. Through summers spent grazing our animals on the steppes, over winters that froze the ground we trod on and chilled our bones, Pa guided us up to the mountains and back again. Who would lead us now?

My brothers Chinua and Gan were ten and seven, still young. Could Ma shoulder Pa's mantle?

The uncertainty I felt about life without Pa hitched onto a caravan on a trail to nowhere. Most unsettling was my doubt. Even though Grandma had forewarned me of the events I'd witnessed; even though she'd cautioned that one after the other our teachers would be taken from us, when truth spoke to me in the voice of an old woman, I was too fond of her face to hear clearly.

Straight away distrust ensnared me, separating me from Pa. What was the purpose of being a shaman if he couldn't foresee his own fate? More to the point, why have a presentiment of disaster when there was no chance of stopping it?

Incandescent, I stretched my arms to Father Sky and wailed. Where were my sisters now that they too were in mourning? And Little Linet? Alone, what would become of her? What would become of us all? I thought of my sisters and yet sobbed for myself, thrashing Mother Earth first with my fists, clawing at her with my nails.

My horse nuzzled me gently while a southerly wind stirred, rustling the long grasses of the steppes. Above me, the hawk was still whirling, and when her shadow grazed me a second time, the heat in my tears cooled. Somehow, hawk, wind and horse combined to ease my distress and despite the insults I'd flung at them, earth and sky conspired to help me.

Once I'd stopped crying, Altan nipped me, urging me to sit up. Bit by bit he persuaded me to stroke him. I was sitting on the ground caressing his forehead, when Ma appeared. She'd been out since late afternoon, scavenging for herbs to season our evening meal. One look at my tear-stained face and she knew something was gravely amiss.

'Are you hurt, Zula?' she asked.

I shook my head.

Her face grew pale. Her fingers tensed, gripping the pouch at her side as her eyes darted, glancing at the dirt on my clothes, my hands and nails blackened from the thrashing I'd given Mother Earth.

'What is it, Zula?'

The bite of tears stung me once again. Unwilling to say the words she had to hear, I covered my face.

Ma looked on and absorbing the fold of my body, the tussle between pain and fury on my face, she asked: 'Has something happened to your father?'

I gagged and my soul sobbed as Ma stifled a scream in her throat. Even so, she sat down, and as she held me, stroking locks of my hair that fell like smatterings of snow over her hand, I howled like a lost wolf cub.

On the day that Pa's body was due to come home, the faint grumblings of a storm hung in the air. Our animals sensed it: the horses were skittish, the sheep unable to graze, while our camels, usually docile, refused to settle. I sniffed the wind and felt prickles of dust in my nose. A fork of lightning flashed across a pale afternoon sky that darkened as thunder rumbled. Then, all at once, a cold wind swirled from the mountains. Whistling over the steppes, it stirred grass this way and that, like a giant's hand would a mighty cauldron. I turned to look at the horizon and saw billows of black clouds. Clouds laden with dust. I called my brothers, Ma as well.

We were dressed in our best clothes in readiness for Pa's arrival: long-sleeved tunics in yellow, folded at the chest over trousers. We quickly took the tunics off, put on our work clothes, and set to.

Thankfully, we each knew what to do. You don't spend years breeding livestock without understanding the hazards involved: drought, ferocious dust storms and freezing cold winters that few creatures survive. Pa once told me that the times we were living through were confused. Nothing was as it should be because the earth was changing; and as it changed it behaved with the unpredictability of an angry child: weeping one moment, sullen the next. A child that spits and rages, stamping its foot at every turn. Wind magic was futile in the situation we found ourselves in. Nothing would soothe the child's lament; nothing could ease its frenzy. And now that Father Sky had taken to hoarding rain high above the clouds, the frequency of dust storms carried over the mountains from China was intensifying.

My little brother, Gan, named for the boldness of his spirit, helped me open the gates of the corral as we started moving our animals behind our gers to shelter them from the storm. Pa's youngest brother, Batu, had joined us the day before. He'd arrived on our pastureland with the ease of a late summer breeze, behaving as if he'd never been away. Struck by how warmly Ma had embraced him, how readily he praised Pa for helping him find a bolthole in the city, I hushed Grandma's whispers in my ear.

My uncle had left that morning with family members of the other men killed in the rock fall to retrieve their bodies. Batu had brought with him a ger and three mouths to feed – his wife, Knenbish, and two small daughters. His ger gave us a second windbreak in the gathering storm, another pair of hands, another set of feet and the quick wits of Knenbish, could make the difference between life and death.

'Hurry, Chinua!' Ma cried.

Chinua, on horseback, hooted at our sheep. He rounded them up and whooping, forced them behind the two gers, where Knenbish and I tried to calm them.

In front of us sinister clouds of dust, rolling in from the mountains, crept closer.

When the sheep were safely in place, I returned to our corralled animals and called Altan. In the throng of horses, I heard his whinny. As soon as he was within range, l jumped on him and, steering him with my knees, drove our horses to where the sheep lay, heads down, eyes closed to the wind.

By now flurries of air blew in blasts, battering the earth flat, rattling at the doors of our homes. And with every gust came the pinch of tiny splinters of grime. They nipped at my ears and crept up my nose, half-blinding and throttling me at the same time.

I tore the strip of cloth I wore around my neck in half. A quick flip and roll and it became a muffler protecting my nose and mouth, and a dust mask for Altan as well. My eyes I kept half-shut.

The storm was almost upon us when the wind rammed the gate shut and slammed little Gan to the ground.

Ma hauled him up and handing him over to Knenbish, said: 'You two, go inside.'

Gan protested but Ma insisted: 'I've no time to argue, son. But if you're as bold as you're supposed to be, make your father proud of you today and do exactly as I say.'

Knenbish dragged him into our ger.

To me, Ma yelled: 'Faster, Zula, we're just about out of time. The camels.'

I galloped back to the corral to round up the last of our livestock. Chinua opened the gate and riding on opposite sides we steered the camels behind our gers. We secured them in a way that created an outer ring with their bodies to shelter the rest of the animals. The reason being that the nostrils, eye-lashes and eyelids of a camel are so wonderfully made, they're better able to filter dust than almost any other creature in the world.

We were nearly done, about to rope them in and run indoors, when a young calf broke loose. Its adopted mother scrambled up, clambering to reclaim him. Chinua managed to calm the mother and hold her in place. Not so the calf. Indeed, the sight of him lurching in the direction of the storm brought Pa's absence closer. In one of the last rituals he'd performed, Pa had coaxed the camel and calf to bond. One had lost its mother, the other a calf, so Pa sang a song to encourage the cow to suckle the waif.

Mindful of Pa's song, its sweetness and lilt, I yearned to hear his voice once again. My heart ached as memory flamed into grief: those low notes of his, the steady beat of his drum. If it hadn't been for the sturdiness of Altan, I would have keeled over and wandered into the storm as distraught as the agitated calf. But Altan steadied me, and I heard Pa speak to me for the first time since his death.

'*Don't chase the calf, Zula, if you chase it you will frighten it even more. Sing to him instead.*'

Despite the clamour, I dismounted and standing resolute, eyes half-closed, I allowed Pa's song to fill me. Then I sang about the love between mothers and their children, about ties that bind and continue down the ages from one generation to the next. Timid to begin with, faltering at times, I almost stopped. But as Pa's presence grew within me, he swept me along and giving my voice wings, it soared. Before I knew it, I was singing a song Pa hadn't had time to teach me: the song that makes camels weep.

The wind must have carried the tune, for by the

time I'd finished, through my half-closed eyes, I saw the runaway calf coming towards me. Behind him, shepherding him home before the curse of dust-laden wind overwhelmed us, was Pa's horse, Takhi.

21

Zula

✳

As the storm was reaching its peak, wind battered our ger determined to bludgeon everything in its path. Usually when the elements assailed us, once our animals were safe, Pa would tell us stories. Without him around, I felt as awkward as I imagined Linet and Adoma were feeling. Awkward because grief makes you heavy; so heavy that from waking to sleeping is like wading through a swamp that swallows you whole. Mindful of every step you take, every word you say, it sucks you in, until you're forced to face the fact that nothing will be the same again.

Mired in pain our pride of three didn't behave as we normally did. How could we when we hadn't had a chance to reconnect, to take stock and plan for our circle. Linet, in particular, troubled me. Suspiciously calm, she was evasive, distracted, while Adoma spent morning, noon and night consoling her grandmother or trying to find the culprit behind Okomfo Gran-pa's murder. I was distraught yet busy at the same time seeing to Ma and my brothers. Out in the pasture, without Pa to supervise us, I made sure our animals were milked and watered. Every day I tried to compensate for Pa's absence by doing more than I usually did.

Outwardly, my hands on Altan's mane and my legs around his girth were constantly in motion. Inwardly, I was drowning. I ached for Pa's steadying hand on my shoulder, his warm gaze and easy praise. Yet much as I yearned for him to be with us again, I was angry and confused as well. How could he and Grandma leave when there was so much I still needed to learn from them, so many questions I needed answers to?

The raging wind rattled the columns that held up the ceiling of our home, tipping it to the left. Huddled by the stove sipping noodle soup we looked up: Knenbish and her daughters, my brothers, Ma and me. Knenbish's youngest, still a toddler, started mew-ling. Knenbish stroked the child's hair, rocking her gently as the girl shivered, expressing what each of us, in our different ways, was feeling: fear that in this our first storm without Pa, our home was about to collapse.

Ma caught my eye and chased fear away: 'See us through this storm, Zula,' she said. 'Tell us one of those stories your grandmother used to tell you.'

I was not in the mood for story-telling. I was about to shake my head and shrug when I heard Pa's voice. *'Go on, Zula,'* he whispered. *'Give it a try.'*

I did what Pa asked. My lips twitched in a smile that kindled the shine in my eyes. Then, with my brothers seated either side of me and Knenbish and her daughters opposite, I started a tale of how the wind when it rages is not the wind as such, but shrieking warriors of the Great Khan, warriors hurling war cries as they gallop into battle.

I was halfway through the story, naming the whoosh and swoop of the elements; halfway through giving wind, dust and lightning familiar faces to help us tame them, when a mighty thump sounded at our door. After a second thump, the door opened.

In came my Uncle Batu. A small, stocky man with a weatherworn face, he was followed by three skin-walkers. Two were tall and bony. The third, broad as a bear with a shaggy mane of brown hair, entered our home with a swagger. Beside Broad Bear was a Mongolian, a city man from Ulaanbaatar, by the look of his coat. My uncle introduced them to Ma, naming the men one after the other: Mr Anderson, Mr Lee, Mr Clements and Mr Atagan, their interpreter.

I watched the strangers closely: watched how they walked, how they talked. Watched as Ma bowed and with arms outstretched welcomed them by placing her hands around theirs. She didn't smile. She looked on them favourably with kindness in her eyes, as is our custom; and in doing so, found a seat for each of them, before I served them tea with milk and a dash of salt.

Tea dispensed, I arranged a plate of dried meat and *boortsog* biscuits, and holding it aloft, my eyes devoured the foreigners while my nose filtered their aroma.

What surprised me was that they stank of sweat the same as we did. But there was something more: of the tall, bony ones, the taller of the two had downy hair white as an egret; the other the eyes of a vulture and hair every bit as black as those scavengers I'd seen feasting on the carcases of rabbits. Both, I noticed, were highly-strung, as skittish as the most nervous of our horses. Their bodies shook before they thanked me, their hands trembled lifting bowls of tea to their lips, and seeping from their flesh was the sour musky scent of deep unease.

The Broad Bear of a man was different. The more I looked at him, the more my heart raced. He reminded me of the enormous brown bear I'd encountered in my soul journey before Grandma fell ill after she'd shouldered a blow intended for me. Seemingly relaxed, the man's sallow eyes hinted at a cold, steely will, while the interpreter, sitting beside him, gave the impression of a sleek, self-satisfied cat; a cat with a tongue adept at lying, whose clothes still held a whiff of city dust. What I saw with my wolf's eyes was that the one thing they had in common were hearts as unforgiving as rock. It was then my mind stirred, hissing and spitting because of Pa and Grandma.

And how they stared, those men! I forget, sometimes, how odd I must look to outsiders with my thunder-snow hair and grey eyes. Unlike our fellow herding families who knew me as Pa's daughter, the skin-walkers seemed astonished by me. Their eyes followed me everywhere. And to be honest, I was tempted to finish them off there and then, to use my gift to dazzle-blind them with a blink of an eye. It would have been easy; too easy and inhospitable. So I bided my time in the hope that soon, I would pick them off one after the other.

Another roar of wind and the columns of our ger creaked again. I had to bite my tongue not to chuckle at the tall strangers, for they flinched, looking around nervously. My eyes locked with theirs and it dawned on me that they were as frightened of the storm as Knenbish's toddler.

Pa would have told them that they were foolish to travel in such weather: dust and wind can bring death to the home of the richest of princes. Pa would have said that it's safer to travel when the wind is with you, not fighting you. Perhaps the storm hadn't started when they'd set off from their camp. Perhaps they were halfway through their journey before the wind began to stir, lashing their vehicle with dust.

What I observed was this: the tall strangers shivering, then pulling up their collars before downing their tea. And while they trembled the Broad Brown Bear and the Cat man gently mocked them. When they'd finished and I'd cleared their bowls away, my uncle invited them to drink some of Pa's vodka with him. They agreed.

That's when they explained to us, through Cat man, how they had happened to arrive late in the middle of the storm. They were on the way back to their camp having delivered the bodies of two of the men killed in the avalanche of rocks. Pa's body was not with them.

Ma's head dropped. She rubbed a sleeve over her eyes to clear them of tears. When she was able to raise her head once again, she asked: 'Why? Why have you not returned my husband to us? His body is all we have left of him and we need to see him one last time.'

'Wife of my brother,' my uncle replied, 'there is a reason for this.'

A flush of anger reddened Ma's cheeks: 'Then tell me!'

'It is what my brother wanted. He instructed those who went with him to the mountains that if any danger befell him they should take his remains to the Giant's mouth and leave him for the eagles there. These men here,' said my uncle referring to the skin-walkers, 'with your permission, are willing to transport my brother, your husband, to his final resting place. Say the word and they will help you fulfil his wishes.'

'I do not know where the Giant's mouth is,' said Ma.

A glint of surprise flitted over Batu's face: 'One of you must know, surely!'

Ma shrugged: 'If it's the place I think it is, it's a dwelling place for shamans. Only they may set foot there: shamans and, at times, their relatives.'

'Well this is such a time,' my uncle replied. 'Zula, do you know where it is?'

My thoughts were far away weaving a story around Pa: his final wishes, his instructions to his friends. So he'd known, after all, of the danger he was in. Why didn't he tell me? Warn me at least? The answer hit me like a slap on the cheek and my weaving ceased. Grandma had warned me, so why should he, especially if he wanted to protect me? I heard my uncle call my name again: 'Zula!'

'Yes, Uncle?'

'Do you know the place where your father wants to be laid to rest?'

I nodded. But as I did, I sensed waves of excitement radiating from Broad Bear and his accomplices. They shifted their stools, inching closer. They came so close I smelled the sulphur on their breath; I saw sparks of delight in their eyes and greed in my uncle's.

What did they want from us? What were these strangers after and why was my uncle helping them?

Unsure of how far I could trust my uncle or how my words would be translated in language the skin-walkers understood, I spoke plainly: 'Weren't you once a shaman yourself, Uncle? In fact, didn't you recognise the man in the mountains before my father did?'

Blood drained from Batu's cheeks.

'Uncle, why didn't Pa and Grandma show you the trail to the Giant's mouth?'

The summer breeze around Batu turned icy as rage thickened his throat. Yet before he gave way to anger, he swallowed it with a smile. 'Don't play games with me, Zula. Answer me when I ask a question.'

I nodded again. 'I know the place well, Uncle, but I will not take these men there. The Giant's mouth is sacred. It is not a place for foreigners.'

Batu snorted. A snort that implied that in his opinion I had no idea what I was talking about and should keep quiet in a conversation that was the preserve of adults. Edging closer to where Ma was seated, he touched Ma's knee: 'Woman, these people have agreed to compensate you for the loss of your husband. If you take them where they want to go as well, they will reward us handsomely.'

Ma looked from Batu to me, her dark eyes searching, anxious. I already knew how worried she was that without Pa we wouldn't be able to survive.

Ma pressed him: 'You say they've agreed to compensate us for our loss?'

An eye on me, the silky Cat man nodded at Ma.

'How much?' I asked him. 'How much is my father's life worth?'

Cat man told us.

My cheeks burned in disbelief. Pa was worth ten times that amount. No, not ten, a million times more!

'And if I were to take these strangers to the Giant's mouth?'

The sum he quoted was double the amount.

With a slight shake of her head, Ma covered her face with her hands. I placed an arm around her, as did Knenbish. And when my little brother Gan tiptoed behind Ma to ask her why Pa hadn't come home yet and when he would return, she shuddered swaying back and forth.

Funerals are expensive here; so expensive that I would be lying if I said I wasn't tempted by the skinwalkers' offer. It dangled before me bright as a jewel. So much money could help us restock our herds as well; help us buy books for school. As it was, apart from over the winter when my brothers and I attended classes at Gobi Altai, we relied on our labour over the summer. With extra money we might be able to fulfil Pa's wishes. He'd wanted my brothers to attend school full time, so they could benefit in ways I hadn't been able to. Now Pa was gone, my schooldays were over.

The possibility of what might be slipped in. I know because Cat man smiled thinking he'd succeeded in persuading me to do the bidding of his masters. Yes, I was tempted, but before I could utter a word, a drizzle of honey and milk sweetened my tongue and my soul shimmered.

The breath of the Sleeping Giant, grazing my skin, swept me into his embrace. The higher he lifted me, the more I tasted milk and honey, and from one moment to the next, I was up in our lair a lone wolf baying in wolf-light. The wind, sharp as a whip's slash, would have hurt if not for the beauty of the setting sun. While around us the air, alive with the swoop and whirl of eagles, sparkled as I howled serenading him in wolf song.

How could I even think of betraying Pa by showing strangers our secret place? There was no chance. I was too far on the shaman's journey. The Giant was part of me; glints of his flint sharpened my blood. I would rather die than dishonour him.

Cat man had smiled too soon.

I shook my head: 'Give us compensation for my father's death,' I said, 'and when the storm has ceased making mischief, you people should go.'

Ma smiled, confirming my request.

The strangers agreed to do what we asked of them. In the meantime, with the storm still shrieking outside, they had to stay.

My uncle poured more tots of Pa's vodka. They drank a second glass, then a third. As the liquor quickened their tongues, the skin-walkers pleaded with Ma and my uncle. They begged them to make me change my mind. Indeed, they increased the sum they'd offered three times over. And when I still wouldn't budge, but gave them a puzzled smile instead, they turned to my uncle.

My uncle nodded. In that single gesture, the dip of his head combined with the hunger on his face, I grasped he was under their spell. Sometimes, I reasoned, in the full knowledge that I'd been enticed as well, the lure of money can make people travel to places most of us dare not venture. In the same way that the strangers realised that what they had to offer me was nothing compared to my love of Pa and the Sleeping Giant, I saw with my wolf's eyes that my Uncle Batu was preparing to betray us.

22
Zula

L ate that night, I was about to sleep when I
    sensed Linet's shadow snuggle against my
    shoulder. I made space for her and shifted as
Adoma wriggled on my other side. I hadn't summoned
them, hadn't called for help. Nonetheless, it was such
a relief having the three of us together again that I
realised how much I'd been missing them.

I wrapped my sisters around me like a cashmere
shawl. And as I felt them warming and thickening my
soul, I began to wonder why we hadn't called each
other, even if just for a moment, instead of allowing
ourselves to be scattered as sand is in a storm. No
matter the circumstances, we should have made an
effort to spend time together.

'*No use crying over spilled milk,*' Nana Merrimore
would have said. Or to use Pa's words: '*Don't roll
up your trousers before you get to the stream.*' My

teachers' voices resonated in me as I lifted, once again, the burden of their loss.

'And Okomfo Gran-pa, what would he have said, Adoma?' I asked.

'*What is done today is done. Tomorrow will be better.*'

'I hope so,' said Linet. 'Things can't get much worse than they are now.'

The three of us, stretched on my narrow bed, reflected on the changes we were a part of. Like butterflies emerging from chrysalises, blood pumped into our wings. And as we flapped and flexed them, unsure of our new place in the world, we touched the wound of our teachers' deaths.

I remembered Pa, recalling his last ritual: that song he sang that caused our camel to weep.

And then Adoma, adding her memories to mine, looked back on a time of laughter: 'Do you remember the day your pa taught us the rudiments of wind magic? I was so eager to learn I conjured a tornado that flung me into the sky!'

'We remember. We remember,' said Linet and I.

'And the time Nana Merrimore took us down to the Linet Lake and showed us the magic that flows in her?'

'Yes!' said Adoma and I.

'And the second time, when unbeknown to our mentors we met there at night,' I reminisced. 'Do you remember how the lake seemed to kiss us as she first held us and then drew us in?'

'We do,' said my sisters before repeating a declaration our teachers had taught us: 'We remember because water, the most powerful element of them all, has memory and remembers us. And whether we acknowledge it or not we remember it too!'

In our shadow world we high-fived.

'Remember that afternoon,' Linet chuckled, 'when Gran-pa showed us how to make fire magic with a flick of a finger? That day when I flicked and flicked and nothing happened?'

'I shall never forget,' said Adoma.

I laughed, my first belly burst of laughter since Pa's death.

'Nothing happened,' Linet continued. 'So Gran-pa says, *"Linet, you should try to do everything you want to do with great intent. You should do it as if you mean to set the world alight with those fingers of yours."* So I do what he says and whoosh! The forest would have burned to the ground if a tear hadn't fallen and turned fire into water to douse the flames.'

I laughed again. And between our laughter and back-slapping, Adoma, black eyes ablaze tossed another memory in our pot: 'Remember the time you took us up to your eyrie in the Giant's mouth, Zula? And bursting with sky magic we flew high-high up, even higher than eagles?'

Linet nodded: 'That's when I first felt the Giant's breath and said: "That Giant of yours, Zula, is alive. He's alive!"'

'We remember, we remember,' Adoma and I replied.

'And I remember your river, Adoma,' I recalled. 'Your sacred river and those days we swam with otters. We'd crawl out on to the river bank slick with mud, the smell of otter on our breath.'

'I shall never forget,' murmured Adoma.

'And Gran-pa's lessons,' Linet went on. 'That weird tingling I felt in my fingers the day he showed us how to channel energy from earth, sky and water to protect our sacred places.'

I nodded and stirring our memory pot, stoked the dying embers of its fire. 'And of all the lessons they taught us, which is the most important?'

We recited the words our teachers had taught us, the basic tenets of our lore from which our knowledge of magic flowed: 'Be still, align your senses with your surroundings and *nsoromma*. Learn to listen. Master your senses: sight, sound, touch and taste. Above all, breathe.'

Our pot full to the brim, Linet said with a sigh: 'Now that they've gone and we're on our own, let's start a new chapter. Let's do things differently, like we decided the other week.'

'Are you happy with that my sister-friend?' Adoma whispered.

'Sure,' came Linet's reply. 'Absolutely fine.'

'Start afresh so soon?' Frowning, Adoma raised an eyebrow.

'Why not? I'm right as rain. Best foot forwards as Nana would say.' Linet laughed: a shrill quiver of laughter that grated.

'I wish I could say the same,' said Adoma. 'The fact is, my sisters, the *wahala* in our house is frying my brains. Gran-pa was murdered and all Sweet Mother can talk about is what sort of funeral we should give him. She wants a Christian burial, of course. So I tell her again and again: "Sweet Mother, Gran-pa's body is on ice in the mortuary. He is now a police case. Under the circumstances, we should be trying to find out who ordered his death!"'

'Do you know who did?' asked Linet.

Adoma nodded, made a gesture that zipped her lips and then said: 'I think I know. And with your help, if we gather every bit of magic in our blood and draw on earth, wind, fire and sky, justice will be done.'

We agreed and yet Adoma continued pressing the bruise that returned her to her mother.

'Now that Okomfo Gran-pa is gone those Alleluia people have taken over our house. They are squatting in every room, I tell you, driving Milo and me mad. And Sweet Mother? She is the worst of them all. If I say "cat", she says "dog". If I say "left", she says "right". Her way of thinking is like fufu is to kelewele. I'm kelewele, plantain juicy and ginger hot, while Sweet Mother is fufu fat *paaaah*!'

'Your mother reminds me of my Uncle Batu,' I admitted. 'Except he's small and stocky, a *hungry* man.' I described the meeting that had just taken place, and as I explained the connection I sensed between my uncle and the skin-walkers, I tried to imagine the many ways Batu could undermine us by revealing the whereabouts of the Giant's mouth, if I took him there. Even so, there was no way I could exclude him from Pa's funeral.

'Show him to us,' Linet suggested.

I held out my hand, and as my sisters touched my tattoo, an image of my uncle bloomed. With it came a waft of his scent.

Linet sneezed. 'Nasty. Very nasty. He uses a veneer of summer to hide his stench. Be careful of him, Zula.'

'Eh-eh! This man is envious,' said Adoma pulling away. 'What he sees he intends to take.'

Their reactions confirmed my suspicions.

'Batu wants more than his fair share of everything,' said Linet. 'So what's in it for those skin-walkers? Why go to all this trouble?'

'They want to find out where the Giant's mouth is,' I replied. 'As soon as they know, they'll investigate to see if there're any minerals up there: gold, copper, coal. Whatever they find, they're after one thing alone: to make as much money as possible.'

'And another thing,' said Adoma. 'Didn't you once say that your pa suspected the Giant's mouth could be the burial ground of the Great Khan?'

I nodded. 'Pa told me that everyone who witnessed the Great Khan's burial was slaughtered to make sure that the place was kept secret and his treasure safe...'

'*Aba*!' said Adoma. 'Once those skin-walkers know the source of your power, they'll know how to control you, like you British did when you stole the Golden Stool of Asante...'

'Not that again!' Linet snapped. 'I wasn't even alive then!'

'Linet, my sister, I'm not blaming you, I'm talking facts. Simple facts. You British conquered us, and after you took the Golden Stool and sent our chiefs into exile, we became your slaves.'

'And so?' said Linet.

Adoma sighed: 'As for you, you are too sensitive! Fact: I am linking my history to Zula's. That. Is. All.'

'Yes, we were conquered,' I agreed, 'yet long ago we were conquerors too. In his day the Great Khan ruled most of the world.'

'Makes no difference,' shrugged Adoma. 'We conquered as well. Fact: Zula, you mustn't let those strangers go anywhere near your shrine! Your Giant won't like it. And if you feel a pinprick of the pain Gran-pa and I felt when our place in the forest was spoiled, your heart will break.'

I trembled at the thought that there were likely to be more explosions where the Sleeping Giant lay. I shivered and sensitive to a change in me, Adoma hugged me, inhaling the scent of my skin: 'A taste of honey,' she said, 'a drizzle of horse milk. Is he calling you again, Zula? Has he taken you up to his lair?'

Linet, following Adoma's example, went a step further. She licked the tender flesh of my wrist above my pulse. Her eyes widened as her mouth opened: 'He has!'

I nodded, marvelling at the intensity of emotion the Sleeping Giant woke in me. At times the breadth and scale of my feelings seemed to fill the sky with rain clouds that after bursting, watered the desert ten times over and then again.

Adoma, named for her wisdom and grace, teased her fingers through my silver hair and for a moment her dark skin against my silver shimmered like a lone zebra on the steppes. Adoma smiled: 'Okomfo Gran-pa used to say that this is how it is for some of us. We love the places we look after so much that when it finally becomes a part of us, it is our everything and we become like husband and wife, wedded for eternity.'

I didn't know how to explain that 'my everything' was now much more than a place to me. What had started out as a strongly-felt presence was beginning to take on the shape of a being that absorbed me completely; a being, who even though engraved in the landscape seemed to have a will of his own, capable of thrilling me at a moment's notice.

I nodded, aware that in a way I didn't completely understand, I was drawn to the being my grandmother had called my man in the mountains. Was it possible to love a place in the same manner as a person? Perhaps it was.

Linet, stroking the soft down of my forearm absorbed my confusion, and marshalling her gift for cutting to the heart of the matter with the blade at the end of her tongue, asked: 'Do you *love* the Sleeping Giant, Zula?'

'I don't know,' I whispered. 'Now that Pa's gone I cleave to the Giant more and more. And when I think about him, I want to be up there close to him all the time.'

'That's how it has always been for you, Zula,' Linet replied. 'The older you've grown, the deeper your love. Maybe that's how it has to be if we're to protect the places we care about. Because if we didn't care *passionately* about them, we'd allow skin-walkers to tear them apart. If there was any hint of fracking anywhere near the Linet Lake, any chance of its water being drained or contaminated, I'd destroy their machines and peck out the eyes of any skin-walker who dared to walk by.'

I allowed Linet's comments to sink in and as I reflected on them, I began to wonder what advantage

I had over my uncle. And if I did, what chance did I have of stopping him from doing what he might be planning?

Catching the drift of my thoughts, Adoma jumped in: 'If you think that he's going to give the location of the Giant's mouth to those skin-walkers, then he's even more of a fool than Sweet Mother!'

'Listen,' I said. 'If my uncle so much as tries to show them the Giant's mouth, we'll have to deal with him, deal with all of them. Are you two with me?'

'Try to stop me,' said Adoma.

'And you, Linet?'

'Sure,' she said airily.

In our shadow world, I brushed against my lake sister and sensed that well within her once again. Only this time it was brimming over with tears.

'What is it, Linet? You're not yourself,' said Adoma, tapping into the jarring sensations that passed from Linet to us.

For the third time she insisted: 'I'm fine, absolutely fine.'

She didn't sound it. Adoma and I circled Linet to gather her in. We tried to draw her closer but she pulled away. She froze, cold as marble, as Adoma crooned: *'Little Linet, Little Linet, child of the Linet Lake.'*

'I am not little,' cried Linet. 'I know how to look after myself.'

Adoma recoiled. Then inclining towards her, probing and listening to Linet with her inner ear and heart, Adoma paused.

'My sister!' she said at last. 'What have you done? Correction. What haven't you done? Have you contacted those people Nana Merrimore told you to?'

Linet's face flushed as she struggled to lie. The lie was not forthcoming, for between us three there is only truth, a truth that is as clear as water for each of us to see.

'No, I haven't had time yet,' said Linet. 'I've been busy.'

'Doing what?' Adoma again, eyes gimlet-sharp like her grandfather's.

'Well, first of all, as soon as I found Nana's bank cards, I had to take some money out and go shopping. I bought food for Bracken and myself. There was so much to do…'

'Does anybody know that Nana Merrimore is no more?' Adoma asked.

Linet frowned, and reluctantly, face squeezed tight in anger, she shook her head. 'If I tell them, they'll disturb the lake. They'll drag it and then not only will they find Nana, they'll find all those other poor souls as well. Those women they drowned because they were witches. I can't have that.'

'Hush, my sister,' I murmured. 'Hush, Linet, hush.' I smoothed her mane of midnight curls and when her head slumped on to my shoulder, Adoma and I cradled her until Adoma asked:

'When are you going to call those people Nana Merrimore asked you to, Linet? Rosie and Redwood. You are going to call them, aren't you?'

Linet remained silent. Then, as her coldness began to thaw and warmth crept into her body, tears filled her eyes: 'I never mentioned it,' she confessed, 'but I saw what was about to happen to Nana. Remember that day when I called you over, and she and her friends were drinking? I saw, but didn't think it possible. Perhaps if I'd talked to her, I mean *really* talked to her, perhaps she'd still be alive.'

'I saw Gran-pa's end too,' Adoma admitted. 'I tried to delay it. Tried to prevent it, but I couldn't. Linet, I don't think you could have behaved any differently with Nana Merrimore. I don't think that anyone could have stopped her.'

The Lake-girl disagreed. 'I should have done more.'

'Me too,' I said. 'Grandma warned me, but I didn't believe her enough for it to sink in. Now it's too late.'

Suddenly, Linet's face crumpled. 'I want her back,' she wept. 'I want Nana back.'

In a bid to console her, to help each of us take our first steps without our teachers, I said: 'Come on now, let's go and release our spirit creatures. Let's light up the world and sparkle with sister-magic!'

So that's what we did. We slipped out from the ger.

As soon as the light of the moon touched our shadow selves, we cast caution aside, transforming into creatures of air and land. Cradled by Mother Earth and Father Sky, we played through the night singing songs that soothed the pain in our hearts. We sang loudly, exuberantly on our staircase to the stars.

23
Linet

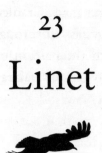

When I open my eyes next morning Nana's name is on my lips. She's there in my heart and mind, and yet for the first time since she left me, I don't turn away from light; I don't close my eyes tight, and curled up in a ball cry: 'Nana! Nana!' again and again. Not today!

Today I hear her whisper: 'That's sister-magic for you! Not only are you swimming in water, you're jumping when you hit the ground as well.'

'Nana, I miss you!' I reply.

Even so, I sit up thrilled by last night. As chuffed as the black-feathered bird within me, a bird red in beak and claw, I smile remembering: Yah! That was me, Linet Merrimore, up there! That was me in the sky swooping and diving. Me sitting on a leopard's head on the steppes. And when the leopard snarled, I knew she wouldn't bite me because the leopard was Adoma. And see that winter wolf dancing in starlight? The wolf with moonbeams around her neck? She won't maul me should I peck at her tail, because that's Zula and Zula's my sister.

Unafraid for the first time in ages, I spring out of bed and racing with Bracken to the lake, I step in.

Bracken meows, nervous that I might take the plunge and do what Nana did. So I say to her: 'Bracken, be quiet. Don't worry. I'm not going anywhere. I'm certainly not going to leave you. Never ever, you hear.'

My hands scoop up water and whirling and turning, I spray it in the air while I sing.

> *'Linet Lake, Linet Lake soft as morning dew*
> *Your Linet-girl is here to play with you*
> *Linet Lake may your day be bright and true*
> *For when wolf-light comes, I'll be here for you.'*

The ripples of the lake become still as a mirror. So still, the birds in the hobbled oaks opposite stop singing. Even Bracken stops screeching as the wind kisses me and then holds its breath. If I'm to talk, this is the time to do so.

I couldn't yesterday because crammed with grief, my throat clenched before I could speak. Today I touch my talisman to gather my thoughts, and say loud and clear so that those hidden beneath can hear: 'Lovely lake, Old Hester, ladies of the lake, especially you, Nana… I wish you could have seen me last night.

I went out with my sisters and each of us changed: one to a leopard, the other a wolf. I grew wings and flew as a chough. Wild, that's me, wild and free. Nana, you should see me now! I'm not frightened any more. Not frightened of the sharpness at the tip of my tongue because that's my beak. I'm a bird, that's me. Nana, if you were here, I'd run to you, and hold you for ever.'

I pause as my conscience pinches, urging me to say more. Lips tight as a clam I'm quiet until the best part of me, the part that listens to my sisters' advice, prises my mouth open: 'By the way, Nana, I haven't got in touch with those friends of yours as I promised. Don't worry I'll call them soon. I might even call them today after I've done what I need to. Bye, Nana! Goodbye, ladies of the Linet Lake.'

My conscience pursuing me, I run back to Carbilly and do what I do every morning. Wash. Dress. Feed and water Bracken. Eat a hunk of brown bread. Down a glass of milk. I'm preparing for the day ahead, when the hairs in my ears prickle and I hear footfall outside.

I pull Bracken to my side and a finger on my lips, catch her eye: 'Shush,' I tell her.

There's a knock on the kitchen door.

Apart from Bracken and I, no one's set foot in Carbilly since Nana's friends came to see her. No one's called her phone or written us a letter.

'Quiet, Bracken.' I dig my hand into a packet of biscuits and take one out. She nibbles it.

A second knock. Then a third. Louder. Determined.

I sniff and catch a hint of Lance in the air.

That blackberry tang tickles my tongue. I swallow. Hold my breath. Berries juice my heart as the bird within me stirs, eager to fly once again.

'Not now,' I groan. 'Please, not now.'

Bracken yawns.

I stroke her neck to distract her from Lance at the door: 'Relax. Good girl,' I whisper hoping that if we can only be quiet enough, Lance will walk away and return when I've concocted a tale to tell him.

Another knock and the door latch rattles. 'Nana Merrimore! Linet! Are you in?'

Bracken meows, breaks free and yowls.

I get up. Too quickly, because I trip on a chair beside me and as it clatters to the floor, there's nothing I can do but shout: 'Coming,' and open up.

Lance is holding a bag. 'This is for you and your nana,' he says, 'apples from Crow's Nest.'

The token around my neck quivers at the mention of Nana's name. My tongue sticks to the roof of my mouth. I try to find my voice, find the right words, but Nana's absence seizes me, and I can barely stand up.

As Lance lurches for my hands to hold me upright, apples tumble over the floor. 'Are you OK?'

I shake my head. He pulls up the toppled chair, sits me down. Yanks its neighbour and while I struggle for breath, searching for a way to explain the predicament I'm in, Lance sits opposite me.

Overwhelmed by grief, I can't hold it in any longer, can't stop the lake of tears inside me from streaming out. The more I cry, the more sobs wrack my body, the firmer Lance presses his hand in mine. Skin to skin, he gradually soothes me while the beat of his pulse steadies my runaway heart. He doesn't ask questions, doesn't pick and probe but waits until the ache inside me subsides.

'Do you want some tea?'

'Water will do.'

After swilling out a glass at the sink, he fills it to the brim.

I gulp it down.

Still no questions, just the gentle graze of his eyes on mine. They're blue, the blue of irises that come up every spring at the lake's edge; fiercely blue with purple glints of kindness. Loving-kindness, Adoma calls it. Even through a kaleidoscope of tears, those eyes do most of his talking for him.

I answer them with words that tear my heart open: 'I'm missing Nana.'

'Is she away?'

'She's gone.'

Again, he waits until I'm able to tell him more. Unsure how much I can trust him, I stick to the facts: 'She's not coming back.'

'Are you certain?'

I nod.

He gets up and one after the other picks up the apples that rolled on the floor. As he places them in a fruit bowl on the table, he looks around, taking in the wreckage in what was once Nana's tidy kitchen. His eyes flit here and there and as I follow them, I glimpse what he's seeing: Nana's sink groaning with unwashed plates, instant noodle cartons on the counter, a half-eaten apple on the table, a hunk of bread I've just bitten into, and beside that open packets of biscuits by a half-used tin of cat food.

He peeps into the sitting room beyond. Piles of paper scattered everywhere. Papers from Nana's writing desk and opened files. Papers and books: all over the floor, on side tables, on the sofa and chairs. I see the mayhem and spinning back to my day of torment, relive what happened.

I watched Nana sucked into the drowning pool. Watched to see if the ghosts there would fling her out like they did me. I waited and waited and when they didn't, I fled into Carbilly in tears and searched everywhere: through Nana's books and papers, notebooks, stacks of bills, invoices and photograph albums. I rummaged through everything I could lay my hands on believing that somewhere in a forgotten corner, she'd have left me a note; a message, at the very least, to explain why she'd left me.

In despair, I hunted through the house: the sitting

room, Nana's study, her bedroom. I looked and found nothing. Not a scribble, not a word to say how sorry she was to leave me. Why not? I couldn't understand why not.

I still can't. I drag myself to the sink and start to wash the plates. When Lance joins me, shadows on his face tell me he's worried.

'Has she really gone?' he asks.

I nod.

'Did she go the way of her mother and her grand-mother before her?'

'What do you mean?'

'Don't you know?' Anxious in case he's said something he shouldn't, he brushes a hand through raven-black hair.

'Know what?' I press him.

'Hasn't anyone told you?'

'What?'

He blinks, turns away and as he does so I remember similar looks and asides directed at Nana and I whenever we ventured into Blisland, our nearest town; asides and whispers I never questioned because they seemed as rooted in our lives on the moor as its granite core: myths about us Merrimores.

A smile hovers over Lance's lips: 'Rumours that's all it is. Old stories and rumours.'

'Go on, tell me!' I insist. I dip my fingers in the sink and flick water at him.

Lance backs away, his smile expanding. 'It's crazy, I know.'

I follow him, spitting water from the tips of my fingers. Water magic. He grabs my wrists and as the warmth of his touch seeps into my skin, I sizzle.

'We're worried in the mind, most of us, I know,' he admits. 'But just about everyone on the moor says Merrimore women aren't born like ordinary folk.'

Hand in hand we rock with laughter. Doubled over, we crumple to the ground. On the cold slate floor, hands light as a feather clasp mine.

'Told you it was crazy but that's the moor speaking. They say you come from the lake out there. And when you're ready to go, you return to it.'

Nodding, I laugh, half-hearing an echo from long ago of words spoken to Zula. Memory rustles through me, and as my voice drifts like a leaf to the ground, I catch it and remember.

'*I'm a Merrimore!*' I said to Zula. '*We're water witches, we are! We're born in water and return to it when we die!*'

I've known this all along, it seems, and yet never grasped the truth of it.

'Is that what you believe?' I ask Lance. 'That I came from the lake out there and when I'm to die, I'll return to it? Am I *that* peculiar?'

Lance shrugs, undecided: 'I did wonder when

I saw you in the mist, but after we went up the tor together...' He shakes his head.

No sooner said, then Nana's phone rings.

I run to pick it up. On the other end is Nana's friend, Redwood. He's with Rosie, just round the corner, and would like to drop in.

I say, 'Fine.'

24
Linet

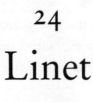

I said 'fine' but in my heart I want to disappear. If I had it in me, I'd say *Abracadabra! Hey presto!* And then *whoosh!* I'd be out of here in a puff of smoke. I'm tempted to use Nana's camouflage trick and blend into the clutter of Carbilly. Merge with the stone slabs on the floor, meld with the enamel in the sink. Best of all would be to swirl around in water and gently slip down the drain, because nothing could be worse than the questions fluttering in my belly. Questions such as: if they're my guardians now, what do they intend to do with me? Will they stay with me at Carbilly? Or try to palm me off on my mother? She can't want me, can she? My stomach heaves. If I could, I would do all of the above and more, even transform into a chough to make my escape. But it's best not to with Lance here.

My heart misses a beat, then starts pounding so

hard I can't breathe. I'm about to bolt when I do what Nana used to do, do what she taught me. I place a hand on my heart, take a deep breath and by the time I've counted to five, the stampede in my chest eases. I exhale, say to Lance: 'Nana's friends will be here soon. I think I'd better clear up the rest of my mess before they appear.'

'Do you want me to go?'

'No! I need your help. You finish cleaning here, while I tidy up the sitting room.'

While Lance flips a cloth in the air, I dart into the sitting room and quickly sort out the papers. Shove them in Nana's desk and close it. Put books back on shelves of the bookcase in Nana's study and then the bigger one in the sitting room. The books neatly arranged, I tidy away photograph albums in a cupboard beneath the stairs where Nana stored them. As I push them in place, of the hundreds of photos inside, one slips out and drops face up at my feet.

Of all the pictures in Nana's album, why does it have to be this one, the one I'd rather not see, that falls out? The one I used to spend hours gazing at until the day came when any patience I had with a woman who never wrote to me, never visited or spoke to me, shattered.

My hand shakes as I bring the photograph closer. The resemblance between the two of us is uncanny. In ten years or so, I'll look more or less like she did:

black curly hair swept up, large eyes with a sheen of shyness and the brightest of smiles that I used to bask in till I knew better. My mother.

I slip the photograph into an album and Lance shouts:

'Linet, your nana's friends are here.'

I return to the kitchen and there they are: Redwood and Rosie.

As soon as she sees me, Rosie opens her arms. I put out my hand to shake hers, but taking hold of my fingers she pulls me in, and before I know it, she's patting my back and crushing me against those bosoms of hers. Whether it's her back-patting or her bosoms that unravel me, I don't know. But from the moment she draws me in to her, palm rubbing my back like Nana used to, I'm undone again. I cling to her as if that rubbing motion is dragging out every morsel of emotion in me: every tear, and between my tears, every sob, and then every piece of my broken heart. She even smells of Nana, for between the mountains of her breasts is a dab of the scent Nana used: a dash of sandalwood with a musky splash of rose.

I cry enough to fill the lake outside. Cry so much that Redwood flaps around me clucking while Lance hands me a dishcloth to mop my face.

'Easy, Linet-girl, easy now,' murmurs Redwood, a big, warm hand on my shoulder.

Rosie steers me to the kitchen table, but like a child bereft, I won't let her go. I can't.

'I need to be by the lake,' I stutter. 'Come with me, Rosie, *please*.' I won't let her go because she reminds me too much of Nana.

Bracken follows us to the Linet Lake, where we settle on my favourite perch for truth telling: a patch of emerald green grass between two granite boulders. Even before we're ensconced, the lake is working its magic on me. Its large expanse the colour of the sky soothes me with the lap and splash of its waves. After the sunshine of early morning, a mist from the moor covers the lake with a hazy autumn shroud: a shroud for Nana, I believe.

Rosie's hands grip mine as, with lazy loops of lake-love coiled around me, I nod at the water and say quickly, before I can change my mind: 'Nana's down there. She gave herself to the lake just before noon on Saturday. That's why I won't live anywhere else but here. This is my home, where I belong. I shall never leave this lake or let the ghosts within her be alone. Do you understand?'

'No one's going to take you away, Linet-girl,' she says. 'Certainly not us.'

'Did you know Nana was going to do what she did?'

'I had an inkling. Especially when she sent me a letter to give to you should anything happen to her.'

'You have a letter? A letter from Nana to me?'

'Yes,' Rosie replies, and slipping a hand in the pocket of her skirt, pulls it out.

I take it. My name, written in turquoise ink, is scrawled on a white envelope in Nana's hand. I bring the letter to my nose. It smells of Nana and a sprig of lavender Rosie must have picked and left in her pocket.

'I shall read it when I'm alone,' I tell her.

And that's what I do. When they've gone and I'm nestled in Nana's chair at Carbilly, I take out the letter.

🐾

Linet, my love,

By the time you get this I'll be gone to my home in the Linet Lake. That's the way it is with us Merrimore women: the lake that flows through our veins splashing magic on us, eventually takes us away. This is how it has always been from one generation to the next until your mother left Carbilly. Remember, Linet, Maya wasn't well. She needed rest and psychiatric care, which, with my help, she received. Eventually, she decided she needed a fresh start, so I took on the role of mothering you to help your gift grow.

Those of us who've guided you, who've helped to forge and teach you, will be gone by the time you read this letter. All three of you will come into your own now. You'll grow and learn from your mistakes. Never forget, this isn't about you, Linet, but a greater good that links every living thing to the source we come from – water: the element that connects each of us through rivers, streams and wells, to the womb of Mother Earth.

Don't be afraid, Linet. I've asked Rosie and Redwood to stay with you whenever they can and watch over you. I've noticed, recently, you've taken a shine to Lance Gribble. If that's indeed the case and he's fond of you as well, don't be surprised if Mrs Gribble pops in from time to time. But remember, always be circumspect about your gifts, and be careful whom you take into your confidence.

Finally, I've left Carbilly in trust for you, and asked Rosie and Redwood to be executors of my will.

My dear, beautiful, wonderful grandchild, I wish you long life and every happiness imaginable. Keep faith in the old ways. May the earth nourish and bless you and your sisters. May the sun smile on your faces and the fair wind that blows behind us all, carry you safely to your resting place.

Your devoted grandmother,

Grizelda Merrimore

25

Adoma

My friend, when *wahala* comes to a house, it is like a bush fire that devours everything in its path: a fire that burns until nothing is left but ashes. *Wahala* sparks gossip at every corner. It catches, blazes down corridors, razes reputations, reveals secrets hidden behind doors, in floors, and walls. Last of all, when what is concealed is exposed, the roof caves in and everything is lost, I tell you! Everything!

This is how it was after Okomfo Gran-pa's murder.

Come and see Gran-ma crying.

Sweet Mother screaming, shaking, running in circles wailing: 'He is dead! He is dead! Our father is dead.'

Wahala when they carried Gran-pa's body inside.

Wahala as panicking street vendors cried: 'Did you see? They shot the old man and straight away the killers' motorbike crashed. That priest, his *ju-ju* must have been powerful – oh!'

Pandemonium. Through the shouting and jostling, I strode to the vehicle I'd dashed to the ground and removed the helmet of Gran-pa's assailant. Eyes still open, life, having fled him, had left in its place a mask of fear. Blood trickled from the side of his mouth.

Even so, I recognised him. His slender face, dark as mahogany, had running down the left side three thin scars.

'*I am Inspector Kaku from Kumasi,*' he'd said in the forest. Inspector Kaku, Mr Lamptey's escort. Now I heard him speaking again, only this time, his voice, a faint hiss in my ear, was that of his frightened shadow:

'My gun! Where is my gun?'

I placed the gun at his side on his chest.

'I am Inspector Kaku of Kumasi,' he said once again. And then remembering those he was leaving behind, he added: 'I have a wife and children to feed. Who will feed them now?'

The shadow sighed, and fading, began his long journey home to the village.

I closed the inspector's eyes and turned as someone called my name.

'Adoma, quick!' The street vendor, who moments before had been roasting corn, was trying to lift the motorbike off the inspector's driver. I grabbed hold of the rear wheel.

'One, two, three,' she said. On the third count, we shifted the mass of tangled metal off the man underneath.

He groaned. I carefully took off his helmet revealing his face. My eyes flared, my jaw fell.

More *wahala*. Mega-full-blue-moon *wahala* as the crowd jeered: 'Nana Junior! What? How be? Eeh! Eeh! Small boy like you dey kill the old man, your uncle? And you the chief's son! *Aba*! Ghana-folk *paaa*!'

Nana Junior, my senior at school, was Granpa's nephew. He opened his eyes and tried to sit up. Collapsed, his head knocking against my knee, I laid him out flat.

A pimple-faced man flung insults at him, calling him the lowest of the low, a disgrace to every family in the village and nation.

Another shook his fist, dashing a foot on the ground as if to grind Junior's spirit to dust. I heard smatterings of lips squeezed in disgust, loud mutterings followed by a cry: 'Let us finish this cockroach off. Because once the police have him the chief will bribe all of them.'

'Kill him,' another yelled. 'Kill him quick.'

Having already destroyed someone that day, I chose not to do so again.

'Help!' I yelled. 'He needs help.'

I looked from face to face searching for a hint of loving-kindness but saw nothing but contempt for the young man who'd helped take Gran-pa's life. I wanted justice as well, but not like this: not street justice, not the lynching of a wounded man. For if Junior were killed, how would I ever find out who had ordered Gran-pa's murder? Inspector Kaku had fired the gun, yet to identify the mastermind behind the plan, I needed Junior alive.

Just as I was about to shield his quivering body from the crowd's blows, someone I recognised elbowed through the crush.

'Kofi, get help,' I bellowed. 'Junior's dying.'

Kofi disappeared.

The mention of death stopped the crowd's advance. Their eyes fixed on Junior's face, they watched him grasp at life's thread with all his strength; watched his fingers slipping, his breath stuttering. Seconds turned to minutes.

'Help!'

Kofi barged forwards, escorting a large woman in a nurse's uniform. Beside her was the street vendor. She bent over, panting.

'Make way! Make way!' my One and Only cried, creating a corridor for Auntie Mina, a district nurse who ran the only clinic in our village.

'You two, hold his shoulders and back,' Auntie Mina commanded. 'I'll take his head. And you,' she said to me, 'take his feet. Lift him carefully! Slowly! Slowly.'

We obeyed and within minutes, thanks to the

speed of Auntie Mina's Toyota, Junior was at the clinic. Luckily for him, the doctor on call was nearby, and once I'd told him that Junior was the chief's son, he did everything he could to save him.

❧

Seven days later, the chief visited our home to grace the one-week anniversary of Okomfo Gran-pa's death. The chief came as a relative, the most prestigious of Okomfo Gran-pa's mourners. And how he came, arriving at dusk with an entourage accompanied by drummers.

We heard them advancing in procession down our road, the drummers marking their progress while the chief's retinue sang a praise song hailing Gran-pa. The song proclaimed Gran-pa's skill with herbs and his knowledge of Ashanti lore that weaves this side of the grave with the one beyond; knowledge that spins a thread back in time to our ancestors.

The head drummer announced the chief's arrival with a drumroll followed by a mighty thump at our gate and a shout of: '*Ago!*'

'*Amie,*' I replied, unlocking our gate and pushing it open.

My task for the evening, Sweet Mother had told me, was to be an errand-girl, a fetcher and distributer of water for our guests. Above all, Sweet Mother said, I was to keep my okra mouth zipped and desist from asking awkward questions relating to Gran-pa's death. We would find out in due course, she claimed. In the meantime I should behave.

Eyes lowered in deference, I nodded meekly when she gave me her instructions. I would have been a fool not to. There had been enough *wahala* already without sprinkling more kerosene on the fire.

As I escorted the chief and his retinue to their seats, as I led the drummers to their positions and handed each of them a sachet of drinking water before the ceremony began, I had a clear idea of what I would do that night, and so did my sisters. Our intention was to identify the spider at the centre of a web of deceit and lies that, having desecrated our shrine, had so inflamed the rage of the goddess of the river that her anger glittered like fireflies around us. Tonight, we'd decided, I would finger the culprit.

My sisters flitted in the shadows around me, slipping between our visitors as nimbly as I did. While up in the highest branches of the neem tree, Milo chattered, peering at those assembling beneath him.

Despite the chief's noisy arrival, from start to finish, Gran-ma was the beating heart of our seven-day anniversary of Gran-pa's death. She was his wife and his business partner, the love of his life, his everything. Seated around her were traditional priests, members of Gran-pa's fraternity, alongside his relatives: his brothers and sisters, their children and then Gran-pa's four children with Gran-ma, Sweet Mother, the youngest, perched on a stool at the end. Gran-ma, alone on Old Freedom, was queen for the night.

After seven days without Gran-pa, she seemed to have shrunk with grief. So much so, that her eyes drifted, searching for the face that would never smile at her again, while her head turned, listening to a voice only she could hear. Restless, she kept dabbing at her tears with a white handkerchief. Gran-ma was distracted. Or so it seemed, until the chief, advancing while dancing majestically under a ceremonial umbrella, paused to acknowledge her. His greasy, *boflot* smile gone, a solemn expression was fixed on his face.

I held my breath, as did everyone present. Having heard the rumours leaping from house to house in the village, how could we not be intrigued? Heads turned as the drumming paused. And when all eyes were on her, Gran-ma shivered as if repelled by the chief's presence. Then, instead of bowing her head to demonstrate that she was filled with gratitude at the sight of him, as a loyal subject should be, Gran-ma snapped into focus. She glared.

My friend, when Gran-ma glares it is not a pretty sight. Her eyes give you a slap you will never forget. A mighty slap, like that of a whip on the cheek; a slap with such fire behind it that grown men feel the sting of tears in their eyes and begin to weep.

She glared, I tell you! Then she slowly stood, shuddered and snubbed the chief by retreating into the house.

Agitation every bit as troubling as an infestation of ants, blighted the proceedings as a chorus of mouths opened and gasped. Like a sudden gust of wind from deep within, disapproval rustled through the gathering.

'Why did she do that?' Linet whispered.

'I think she suspects what I do,' I replied.

'How?' asked Zula.

'Gran-ma's not stupid. She may look it when she stares into her pot of pebbles, but she sees things in it, and more often than not comes to the right conclusion.'

I felt the turbulence in the gathering deepen, settling into our bones as the fracture in the family widened.

I heard someone say: 'This is Junior's fault. This is all his doing!'

Others, grunting in agreement, shook their heads, while to my sisters I said: 'By the time we're done tonight, unless we mess up big time, everyone will know exactly what Gran-ma's thinking, and they'll know that she's right.'

I'd spent the first two days and nights without Gran-pa taking turns with my One and Only in haunting Auntie Mina's clinic, keeping an eye on the comings and goings of the only private room available there; the room in which Junior, according to Aunt Mina's nursing assistant, Sister Mabel, slipped in and out of consciousness. He was so ill, in fact, no policeman came to interview him about what he was doing driving the man who murdered Gran-pa on the back of his bike. No, instead Junior's mother, the chief's third wife, kept guard over him. But even the most watchful of guards, like the hardiest of warriors, has to respond to nature's call eventually.

By the second day when it was my turn to be on the look-out and Kofi returned home to sleep for a few hours, it became clear from the gossip we'd gleaned that the chief was about to have his son whisked to Accra for an operation Junior needed urgently. Death, an elephant pounding at his door, was about to rush in and crush him. Or so Sister Mabel told me.

'What should I do?' I asked my sisters.

'Stay put,' said Linet. 'Something will give soon.'

'Yes,' said Zula. 'The fish sees the bait not the hook. Try to be as patient as a fisherman, Adoma.'

I took their advice and with Kofi's help waited. The more I waited, the greater my suspicion that Junior's family wanted him out of the way. Having an accomplice to murder for a son is embarrassing.

Rumours spread like an attack of fleas through the village: fleas that jumped from house to house, body to body, leaving everyone scratching, while a cauldron of anger about what was happening to our river started tipping over.

'Have you seen them?' people asked. 'The chief and those *galamsey* strangers from out of town?'

'They've destroyed our shrine and now the river goddess is angry,' grumbled another. 'Now we have to buy water. That boy, the chief's son, Junior, is rotten to the core!'

Just before midday on the second day, Junior's mother left his side.

I slipped into his room, turned the key in the lock, and bolted the door.

Junior was wide awake, lounging on the bed, sipping from a can.

If this was indeed a man on the verge of death, I was worse than stupid. I was a downright fool with a brain smaller than a grain of rice.

Junior was so absorbed in playing with his phone that he didn't even notice me.

'Hi, Junior,' I said.

He managed to tear his eyes from his device and froze.

The can dropped to the floor. I picked it up and sitting on his bed, placed it on a locker beside him.

'Yes, it's me,' I said. 'Okomfo Gran-pa's shrine-girl. *Chale*, how be?' I forced a smile, assuming a friendship that had never existed.

'Adoma. What are you doing here?'

He looked at the door.

I showed him the key in the palm of my hand. As he lunged for it, I closed my hand and smiled.

'Foolish girl!'

'After what you did, you call me a fool, Junior? You're the only fool I see here.'

'You this small girl, leave me in peace, Adoma.'

'My friend, I saved you!'

'And so?'

'My brother, if it hadn't been for me, the crowd would have lynched you. You owe me, Junior. If you don't tell me what I want to know...'

'You'll do what, Adoma? Small fry like you, breasts as flat as your back – you think you frighten me?'

His mouth open, he laughed like a self-important beetle that laughs so much it topples onto its back. Except Junior didn't topple. He crumpled onto his pillow, wiping tears of laughter from his eyes.

I stared at him. 'I may be smaller than you. My front may look the same as my back, but you should not laugh at me, my friend.'

I felt a tingling in my fingers and as fury coursed through my blood to my brain, I flexed my wrists. 'If you don't want me to run outside and tell everyone I see how well you are,' I said, 'so very well and hearty, in fact, that you can't stop laughing at me, you'd better talk to me, Junior.'

His eyes hardened.

'You want me to curse you for my grandfather's death?'

He shook his head.

'Then tell me what I want to know! The river goddess demands it. And so do the gods of the forest. Gran-pa's spirit won't rest until you tell the truth. And if you don't tell me, I shall hurl a curse on you so powerful that within a few hours you shall be talking to Okomfo Gran-pa himself.'

A teenager against a young man such as him, the chief's youngest son, should have been no contest. But a guilty conscience can make all the difference. Remember I told you that I only have one friend? Kofi Agyeman is my One and Only for a reason. You see, we Ghanaians are a superstitious people and if there's a single lesson that Gran-pa taught me well, it is that fear of death can be used to powerful effect. *Psychology*, Gran-pa called it.

So I did what I sometimes do when anyone is tempted to laugh at me. I gave Junior my most ferocious shrine-girl stare, the one that glazes my face with an otherworldly sheen and suggests that if the person I'm looking at is not careful, I shall become possessed. In which case, the spirit of the goddess will rush out of me and claim my intended victim.

And so it was that slowly, slowly, I began to sway and then totter as my eyes swivelled up revealing the whites. I raised my hands. The curtains billowed as circles of air spun through the room filling it with wind magic. The windows shook, wood in the frames creaked. Papers flew off Junior's locker. A book rose in the air and then crashed at the foot of his bed as a stench of fear saturated the air.

'In the name of Jesus!' Junior screamed. 'Go away, Adoma. Go away, you devil! In the name of Jesus...'

My eyes back to normal, I kissed my lips: 'You think Jesus hears the cries of a coward such as you, when like me you never set foot in church? No! You believe in the river goddess, Antoa Nyamaa, and she's angry, very angry at the damage you and your friends have done to the forest and her river.'

My hand raised, I directed a blast of wind at Junior's face. He quaked.

'Tell me! If you want to live, tell me now, who was behind Gran-pa's murder?'

Like the coward he was, Junior told me everything.

26
Adoma

Sometimes, when the intent behind a deed is too sinister to put into words, the only way forwards, the only way to breach a web of lies is through action. My sisters beside me, I waited patiently for the right moment to reveal what I knew.

While I waited, I ran back and forth from the kitchen fetching and handing out soft drinks and beer. I ran to and fro carrying paper plates loaded with small chops: fried plantain and roasted peanuts, biscuits and cakes. I gave extra portions to Kofi and his mother, who halfway through the event, passed by to pay their respects.

'Are you going to go through with your plan, Adoma?' Kofi whispered.

'Of course, I am.'

'Be careful,' he said, squeezing my hand.

When the drummers, recharged, started beating their drums again, and the head drummer tapped out my name, the only choice I had was to obey. I was Gran-pa's shrine-girl, a steward to the river goddess, and when the drums speak to me, commanding me to do the bidding of my mistress, I have to answer. And so, to Sweet Mother's dismay, arms outstretched, I stood up.

'Adoma! Sit down!' she hissed.

'Let the girl dance,' cried an old priest, a good friend of Gran-pa's. 'She was Okomfo's shrine-girl, even closer to him than a daughter.'

I took to the floor, and as I did so, I felt the tug and pull of the drum's song as the chief drummer tested my footwork. The drum gave me its rhythm and then my feet followed, while in front of the drummers, three young women, dancers as well, shook gourd-shaped rattles. And as the beads on them jangled, the drummers pounded with the deadly precision of a leopard hunting her prey.

Sweet Mother had told me not to ask awkward questions and I wasn't going to. I wasn't going to utter a word. Instead, I would dance what I knew to be true in front of the chief and the village. And now that Gran-ma, back on Old Freedom, was nodding in approval, I believed the gods were on my side. Is it any wonder therefore, that as I moved my body in a fluid motion of an antelope feeding and drinking at dusk, I heard Gran-pa say: 'Good girl, Adoma. Good girl.'

I was performing the *adowa*, a funeral dance, and with every gesture I made I spoke. *I am an orphan*, I said first of all, a fist clenched against my stomach. *I am bereft. My grief is so great I am like a warrior at war. My heart is broken. I am at war.*

I teased out the dance and as my feet stepped as delicately as a horned creature through grassland, my neck swayed looking this way, then that. Straight away, the drummers followed me, keeping time with the rhythm of my feet. They pursued, even as a part of me stepped aside to allow another entity to enter my being. I quivered, charged with earth and water magic, the movement of my feet on the ground linking me through wells and streams to the sacred river I cared for. I looked down on myself and observed the body of a young woman in black infused with the fearless power of the river goddess. Her strength rippled through my muscles directing the liquid grace of my arms as she posed questions a teenager would never dare ask of a chief.

I danced before him in full view of his entourage, half-aware as I did so, that his face was as thunderously dark as the black funeral cloths we were both wearing. I danced, while tight-lipped, the chief shifted in his chair. He had to stay to watch what the river goddess was saying. Because by now, my body was her home and the gestures I made were hers and hers alone. Nonetheless, as I swayed and my neck dipped, I realised I was knocking on danger's door, and when the door swung open, there would be no closing it again.

'You slaughtered the old man, my priest,' I signalled. 'It was you, chief, who killed my old bull elephant. I will come for you. For with every deed there is an outcome and your time has come.'

Using my arms, my body, the fierce expression on my face, the goddess motioned: 'All of you here, each and every one of you should bear witness to the fact that this your chief must go. And with him must go the foreigners and their *galamsey* workers. Once they've gone, and the river is restored, the village will be strong again. If you allow the river to weep tears of blood, the earth also will bleed, and then you might as well eat dust. Because when the earth bleeds, she dies. Surely, surely, as the sun ushers forth the day, if the earth dies, all of you here will die too.'

Sweet Mother, horrified by what she called my 'child-ish, attention-seeking antics', would have driven me out of the house if hadn't been for Gran-ma. When I came out of my trance, Gran-ma's hand was in mine and she smiled at me – the first smile she'd given a soul since Gran-pa's death. I could tell as I gathered my wits and stretched, that she was pleased. So too were the chief's drummers and most of his entourage.

As for the chief himself, he'd left, claiming that I was an impudent village girl. I was not 'correct'. I should leave immediately and return to Accra with my mother. He, the chief, would not tolerate my craziness a moment longer. So I was told. But from what I could see, he could scream and shout as much as he pleased, because after what Junior had done, nobody was inclined to listen to him. Indeed, it appeared that more than half the village approved of the river goddess' disdain of his leadership.

That night, the moon a waxing crescent, was a curve of luminous light in the sky. As soon as the house was quiet, my sisters and I clad in our shadow selves slipped out. The moon freckled us with glimmer and as we ran through the village screaming with laughter, we untethered our inner creatures. Hands and feet became paws, shoulders sloped, skin and hair matted, enfolding bodies in a blanket of fur: leopard, dark-spotted sleek and white, then a winter wolf, silver bright, fur double layered – inside warm and soft, outside coarse and long. And our teeth! What teeth we animals had, razor-sharp and strong.

As for our sister-bird, tongue and mouth became a beak. Raven curls feathered, arms turned into wings, and with wings flexed, the chough flew. While leopard and wolf, the earth springy beneath our paws, padded, then danced beneath the crescent moon.

After midnight, guided by dark tentacles of night we crept into the chief's compound and sniffed out his bedroom.

He tossed and turned and when at last he sat up, he saw the three of us: a leopard, a red-beaked black bird on her head, and beside the leopard, a winter wolf, eyes moonstone-bright.

The chief blinked, rubbed his eyes. Blinked again.

I snarled taking great pleasure in revealing the length and breadth of my open jaws. I snarled a second time and then yawned while beside me the winter wolf sat panting.

When my leopard mouth opened a third time, I spoke in a voice I knew well; an old man's voice molten with rage, Gran-pa's voice that would live in me until I drew my last breath.

'It is time for you to go. It is time for you to hide your face from this village and leave us for ever. I command that before the cock crows, you and your family leave this village never to return. And should you come back, the curse of Antoa Nyamaa will be on you and your descendants for ever.'

The chief heard us, and as far as my sisters and I are aware, the man who ordered Gran-pa's murder was never seen in the village again.

Our mission in the village complete, my sisters and I, hidden by shadows, retreated to the ruins of the goddess' forest shrine. To honour our decision to shape our destiny as children of the sky, determined to sabotage the activities of skin-walkers, we destroyed every sign of their presence on the river. Standing by the boggy sludge they'd created, I blasted their wooden barricades, using energy from earth, wind, sky and fire. My mind balled in a fist, I smashed their equipment into pieces. As soon as everything was demolished, the wood splintered, then burned, the river started trickling in runnels, till eventually it streamed over mud.

As the river began to surge, as it poured down its main channel, silting roots of shorn trees, as it seeped deep into the soil, we heard it gurgle in satisfaction. Then, gathering momentum, it gushed in a scream of liberation.

Eager to fulfil her promise to flush it clean, Linet raised her hand and drawing on the lake of tears within her, let a teardrop fall on her skin. The moment it touched her, torrents of water cascaded from her palms. A lake-full of water, an endless stream of it, which Zula and I added to as best as we could.

Zula ruptured the sky with a flash of lightning. After a second flash, dark clouds rumbled and as they broke open, huge drops of rain fell cracking like eggs on the ground.

What with the rain and Linet's skill in water magic, before long what had started off as a dribble turned into a flood, an outpouring from Linet and the sky. Drenched, water still trickling from her, Linet stopped, exhausted. If not clean as yet, we knew that the river was in a better state than before. Mother Earth would repair herself in due course, but with our help, she would do it quicker.

27

Zula

P a used to say that among the wisest of the Great Khan's sayings was this: *Only a fool fights a battle he knows he cannot win.* 'So, you and your sisters,' Pa chuckled, 'should choose your battles well. Study your enemy carefully. Get to know him. Learn his weaknesses. And when you're ready, destroy him completely! Half measures simply won't do, Zula, my daughter. You have to be as ruthless as skin-walkers are with us, if you want to defeat them.'

On the day I recalled those words, the day we said goodbye to him, my intention was clear: to give him the funeral he'd asked for at the Giant's mouth. But champing close behind in my mind was my pledge to keep the only safe path to the location secret. After two hours of arduous trekking, we were almost there:

Ma, my brothers, and Pa's siblings – Batu, the youngest and Bataar, the second of Grandma's sons. Pa had been the eldest. Travelling with us on our climb were two of Pa's fellow campaigners and our horses.

On the first stage of our journey, Takhi carried Pa's body cocooned in a fur blanket, upwards, along a track that led through a pass on to a ledge. There we dismounted and tethered our horses. Takhi, aware that this was the last service he would render his master, whinnied as Pa's comrades lifted him off his back on to a makeshift stretcher. His tail swishing, he pawed the ground, while Altan, suddenly skittish, nipped me.

'Don't you want me to leave you, my friend?'

My horse neighed, and with one hoof scraping thin mountain soil, snorted to keep me with him.

'We'll be back soon,' I reassured him. 'Once we've prepared Pa for the eagles, I'll be back.'

I stroked Altan's forehead and blew my breath onto his muzzle to calm him, even though I knew that what he felt, I did too. There was a whisper of unease in the air that hinted all was not well in our group.

Our horses behind us, we continued the climb to the Giant's mouth. Step by step, as I led the procession that carried Pa's body higher, I continued a conversation with him to keep his spirit abreast of what we were doing: how far we'd reached on our journey; how much further we still had to go. I marked the passage of time for him and described the landscape to make sure he understood we were taking him to our shaman home.

I led, my brother Gan's hand in mine, while the others followed on the trail I first walked seven years before. I'd made the same journey many times since, often several days a month in high summer. And yet on every occasion, whenever I approached the Giant's mouth, my heart thrilled at its wild beauty: those vivid peaks and gullies that heralded new adventures: time in wolf-light with my sisters, flying with eagles in their eyries; and time alone, the Giant's breath mingling with mine, his pulse the steady beat of my heart as he drew me ever closer.

'Do you remember this place, Pa?' I asked his spirit. 'It was here, seven years ago, that you lifted me on to that ridge there. And after heaving yourself up, you led me down that path.'

I lifted Gan up, and we descended the footpath, a steep canyon on one side, a granite promontory on the other.

'It was here, Pa,' I reminded him, 'that I slipped and would have tumbled if you hadn't caught me and held me close. Do you remember?'

I sensed the tenderness of Pa's smile on my face, and as I clasped my little brother's hand firmly, I heard once again the slip-slop of a child's tread on wet rock from long ago.

'We're almost there, Gan,' I said to my brother, repeating the same words of encouragement my father had given me. 'Almost there.'

I stopped to look back at the procession behind us. And once again I saw my Uncle Batu surveying the landscape we walked through: the high mountains, ravines and wildwood. Everything he gazed on he seemed to ogle at. Eyes scavenging, his expression ravenous, he looked like a skin-walker about to make a claim on land he already considered his own. Even at a distance, the stench he gave off of fish and seaweed reminded me of a craving for salt. Once the taste is on your tongue, never satisfied, you want more and more.

I watched him, and saw with my wolf's eyes that as soon as my uncle got his bearings, as soon as he memorised visual indicators, he laid down physical markers of his own when he thought no one was looking: a clutch of stones from his pocket, a feather jammed between rocks, the slash of a blade on a tree. How carefully he peppered our trail with signposts he believed no one else would notice.

'Do you have the strength to see this through, Zula, my daughter? Do you have the strength to grab your foe by the jugular and then tear him apart? Are you listening to me, Zula? If you are, answer me!'

'I'm listening, Pa. I'm listening,' I replied.

'And what is your answer?'

'I'd like to say that when the time comes I'll have

the strength to do what I must. But in truth, Pa, my temper is not as hot as Adoma's and my tongue not as sharp as Linet's.'

'Then you will need their help, my daughter. Otherwise, before you know it, I'll look back on my journey through death and see you walking behind me.'

Pa's words forced me to delve into myself to consider questions I'd been pondering but hadn't yet been able to answer. Did I have the heart to deprive Knenbish of a husband, and her daughters, their father? In the weeks I'd known them, I'd grown fond of my aunt and cousins. Come to think of it, even Batu had his good points. Yet the question dangled in front of me like a noose. Was I capable of killing my uncle and anyone else he brought here to preserve the sanctity of the Sleeping Giant? No, I decided. Not in my human form when my victim's eyes could plead with me, reminding me of those of his daughters. Those eyes would haunt me for ever! But as a wolf I could shake him by the throat and tear out his heart without a moment's hesitation.

We trudged higher and higher, deep into the mountain. Gan's footsteps faltered, his hand dragged in mine, while with every step I took that brought our destination nearer, the Giant's breath became sweet and moist as buckthorn berries as he drew me closer. I saw him in the rugged terrain around me; in shafts of clear mountain air, lanced by the sun. I heard him in the swish of trees in the gullies below, in a wild cat's hiss and yelp as it was chased by a fox. And when eagles, talons clawing clouds, circled above us, my heart pounded as when I first felt his kiss.

At the turbulence of wings overhead, Gan shrank into my trousers and hid his face.

'Don't be frightened, little brother,' I said stroking his hair. 'Those birds think we're here to steal their eggs and eaglets. We're not, so they won't hurt you. You're with me and the eagles here know me well.'

We turned towards the crater, which from a distance formed the Giant's mouth and then, one after the other we walked to the cave overlooking the gully of crags and gorges. There, with the help of my brothers and uncles, I built a pyre of stones. And it was on that pyre, his body washed and oiled by Ma, that we children said our goodbyes to our father, my uncles their brother, and his fellow herders, their shaman and friend.

When it was my turn to bid him farewell, I bowed my head in awe at the stillness of Pa's face, engraved for ever in my mind. He was gone. Yet present within me always, I would continue hearing his voice in mine. I would continue feeling the whisper of his breath on the hairs at the back of my neck, urging me on. Though no longer with us, I believed our teachers would never leave us: Grandma, Pa, Nana Merrimore, Okomfo

Gran-pa. Between them they'd formed a bridge my sisters and I had walked on, a bridge linking the past to the future.

'I love you,' I told Pa placing my hand on his. 'I'll always love you.' Then, I added: 'You most probably know this already, Pa, but I'm in love with this place and the being who dwells here. Am I wrong in thinking that the Giant is not asleep but wide awake? Am I mad to love someone I cannot see but feel whenever I look around me? How I wish you were still here, Pa, to answer my questions!'

I heard Pa's voice in the wind. First as a rumble, then a growl that, frolicking around my feet and ankles, whirled around me until it brushed my cheeks in a final embrace: 'Zula, my child, if there is one thing you should remember it is this: there is no right or wrong way to love. Love takes you where it will. From the hour of your birth when I saw the constellation of stars and glimpsed Venus turning to Jupiter, I knew that it was within you to achieve a feat I have not been able to: feel the Sleeping Giant's breath. With breath is life. If you want, you can wake him, Zula.'

Once Pa's words had settled in my heart, I ceded my place at his side to my mother. It was her turn to say goodbye.

Tracing the contours of his face with a hand, Ma said: 'Husband of mine, I am like that old horse of yours, Takhi, at a complete loss without you. Were it not for our children, I would have run into the desert and tried to find you again as he did. But even Takhi couldn't find your trail to the underworld and returned home without you. So now I shall ride him for you, my husband. And whenever I do, I shall listen for your voice in the desert wind and look for traces of your face in the sky. Travel safely to your new home, husband. But remember, no matter where you go, your first home was here with me.' Her right hand on her heart, Ma turned away from Pa and followed me on our steep descent back to our horses.

Two weeks later, when Pa's body had been picked clean to the bone, I saw with my wolf's eyes that my uncle was about to make his move. I hastily summoned my sisters and that night we met at the Giant's mouth at the entrance of the cave.

Our legs dangling over the edge, my sisters and I talked in wolf-light, devising a strategy to keep Batu and his skin-walkers at bay. In front of us, within the croon of a westerly wind, were eagles tending their young. The occasional bleating of a wild goat punctured the calm as I outlined a plan: 'If they come during the day, we can ambush them here and here.' I pointed at two marks I'd drawn on a map scratched on the ground. 'This ledge is where they'll have to dismount if they come with horses. We can frighten them away here as well.' I indicated a spot further along the steep trail where an unsuspecting intruder could easily fall to his death.

'And if they come at night?' asked Adoma.

'We unleash our creatures on them,' I said.

Linet nodded. 'I get the feeling you'd like us to sort them out at night, wouldn't you, Zula?'

'Batu's my uncle,' I explained. 'Knenbish, his wife, is my friend, and her children are my cousins. I don't think I've got the stomach in daylight to eyeball Batu and dazzle-kill him.'

'Not even for your man in the mountains?' asked Adoma.

I frowned: 'If I have to, I can dazzle and blind, make a man miss his step and fall to his death. But with my uncle, I don't know.'

'No one said life would be easy. That's what Nana Merrimore would say,' said Linet. 'Let's hope they come at night then.'

'That's unlikely.' Adoma examined the map between us before her eyes locked with mine. 'To follow the trail Batu laid, they'll need as much daylight as possible. If I were them, I'd start early, and if necessary be prepared to spend a night in the cave before returning next morning. Why create more *wahala* when the expedition is dangerous enough already? No one in their right minds

<207246</207>

would attempt a climb such as this at night. We should set our creatures on them during the day, if we have to.'

'Sounds like a plan to me,' Linet confirmed. 'Let's set the traps.'

So that's what we did. At strategic points along the trail, we prepared snares that could make the difference between life and death: a boulder perched above the track, which with a slight push could tumble down, flattening anyone below; a thin tripwire, invisible to the untutored eye, which could precipitate a fatal fall. We littered the climb with snares to ensure that wherever the trespassers turned, their lives would be in jeopardy for having dared venture so far.

Satisfied that we were prepared for them, we sat and waited for Batu and the skin-walkers.

'My sister squad, how be?' asked Adoma inviting us to nestle and share.

Linet smiled and then laughed in a drizzle of glee that urged us closer still. I sensed a lightness in her that intrigued me.

'How are your guardians?' I asked.

'They're nice,' said Linet. 'They give me money for food every week, pay my bills and visit. Now that Nana's gone, the lake's more of a mother to me than ever.'

'The lake's your mother,' I laughed, 'while this mountain here is...'

'Where your heart is,' said Linet.

'And where your heart resides is where you feel most alive,' Adoma concluded.

'I'm most alive with the lake and Lance,' Linet smiled.

In the glow of the setting sun, Linet's features rippled, a shimmer of light on water.

I nodded as on either side of me, my sisters, each with a hand in mine, thrilled at the Giant's breath. Captivated by and immersed in his splendour, the three of us watched the flight of eagles over his mouth while down below wind whistled, spiralling between crags.

'He's alive and he's waiting for you, Zula,' said Linet.

I chuckled at her fancy, which encouraged mine, for in my heart I felt him draw me even closer. So close that his breath, warm as a sun-kissed feather, tickled my face teasing me.

'I feel him too,' said Adoma. 'You may not be able to see him, Zula, but your man in the mountains is as true as my goddess of the river. He's here, there and everywhere.'

'And what about you, Adoma?' I enquired. 'Any news of Junior?'

Adoma grunted: 'As soon as the chief left us and was no longer a chief, what the police in our village refused to do, they did in Accra. Come and see, operation or no operation, they swoop into Junior's hospital room and grab him like this.' Adoma enacted

Junior being hauled away by the neck. 'And all because a man without power is as helpless as a grain of rice in an anthill.'

That night the three of us slept in my cave at the Giant's mouth. Next morning, I sat up and, alert to trespassers, sniffed the air. I detected nothing unusual. Nonetheless, a moment later, I shivered with the intensity of a child about to come down with fever.

I woke my sisters. 'Something's not right. Do you feel it?'

Linet nodded. 'A sensation like an itch on the skin?' she asked.

'Yes, indeed. There's a sizzle of electricity in the air,' Adoma confirmed. 'Come closer, Zula.'

Adoma touched the tattoo on my wrist. Linet did the same and between the three of us we saw what I couldn't on my own: my Uncle Batu, with four skin-walkers beginning the ascent of the Sleeping Giant. Behind my uncle was Mr Anderson, Mr Lee, Mr Clements and Mr Atagan, their interpreter, each of them armed. The Egret, the Vulture, the Broad Bear, and the self-satisfied city Cat.

'Why's your uncle wearing your pa's white shaman smock, the one with all those tiny mirrors on it?' asked Linet.

I looked again. Sure enough Batu was wearing Pa's special robe of mirrors. The robe sparkled dewy bright, alight with Pa's psychic power. As I stared at it, spasms of fear and anger shook me.

Adoma whistled. 'The cunning dog. He's trying to protect himself! He knows he and his skin-walkers have no place in a sacred space such as this.'

'They're here with murder in mind, Zula,' said Linet. 'They want you out of the way as a first step to taking what they crave from the Giant: minerals.'

'I wouldn't bring them here, so they want me out of the way?'

'Yes,' said Adoma. '*Aba*! These people have no idea who they're messing with. And there you were being dopey-eyed about your uncle. If we don't sort him out now, he's going to be the end of you, Zula.'

'Let's do it,' I replied. 'Let's keep my man in the mountains safe.'

28

Zula

✶ ✶ ✶

If our teachers had been with us, I'd like to think they would have reminded my sisters and me that even the best-laid strategy does not always go to plan; and that at times, there's no other way out but to improvise. We were young, determined to prove that despite our years we could outmanoeuvre five grown men armed with rifles. After Adoma's success in naming and shaming the man behind Okomfo Gran-pa's murder and Linet's affirmation of her love of the lake, we thought ourselves remarkable, which we were. After all, we had magic on our side and our cause, we believed, was a just one.

'Let's find a place above the ledge where they'll have to dismount,' I suggested. 'Then we'll not only know when they're close, we'll see what they're doing as well.'

'Where we laid the first trap?' asked Adoma.

I nodded and using our understanding of animal lore, we called for assistance from the world of the pebble toad, a creature that runs from its enemies by curling up like a ball and throwing itself off the side of mountains.

> *'Pebble toad, pebble toad,*
> *We call on you.*
> *Help us leap and bounce*
> *As easily as you do!'*

We didn't curl up, and we didn't bounce. We weren't running from our enemies, but towards them. Connected to a shape-shifting world we were a part of, the three of us leaped, vaulting down the mountain with the resilience and speed of a tumbling toad. Instead of taking an hour to reach our destination – a boulder on a ridge a few metres above the waiting place for horses – we arrived in less than five minutes. The trespassers were still some distance away. Nevertheless, I heard the steady clop-drop of hooves climbing upwards, ever upwards.

'It sounds like an army down there,' said Linet.

I listened: 'There are five horses with them at least. Batu must have borrowed Pa's stallion, Takhi. He knows the route here as intimately as the sound of Pa's voice.'

Clever Uncle Batu, I thought to myself. As cunning

as a fox, he was every bit as dangerous as a rabid one. And to think that I had hidden Altan at the foothills of the mountains in the belief that to tie him up below would give my presence away. My uncle already knew my whereabouts and was preparing to hunt me down. My one advantage was he had no idea my sisters were with me.

Adoma, ahead of us, stopped at the boulder we'd manoeuvred in such a way that a small push would set it rolling down to the spot where seven years before, if it hadn't been for Pa, I would have fallen to my death. We hid behind the boulder and waited.

About an hour and a half later we heard Batu's party dismounting. The horses tethered, the five men continued the climb on foot. We didn't have to watch them. Not at all, not when we could smell their advance and hear the trudge-heave of men's feet in boots plodding up the slope.

My uncle's instincts were good, I observed, for by the time the men hauled themselves onto the narrow ridge that led to the next stage of the climb, he'd ceded his place at the front to Mr Clements, the Broad Bear.

Broad Bear walked with the strut of a man used to pitting himself against the elements and winning. He moved quickly, confidently, mocking the caution of his fellow skin-walkers who preferred to climb at a more measured pace.

Turning, he bellowed: 'Buck up, you lot. I want us to be up and down by teatime at the latest. We're not on a Sunday school picnic here.'

He turned to hurry them on and in that moment, his back to us, Linet, Adoma and I pushed the boulder. It wobbled. That was it. We pushed again. Nothing.

'Wind magic,' I muttered. 'Let's use the wind to shift it. Quick, my sisters, let's do what Pa would do. When human strength fails, harness the wind.'

Standing side-by-side, breathing in time, we flexed our wrists and when the nerves in our fingers started tingling, we channelled the power of wind and sky to dislodge the boulder. The heavens opened and, tunnelling through, a tornado thundered down. Our arms outstretched we guided it in the direction of the block of stone in front of us. The rock shook, and as its centre of gravity shifted, picking up momentum, it toppled.

'Watch it, Clements! Behind you!'

Broad Bear looked, saw the rock rolling down the ridge towards him and realising there was no space either side of it to escape, twisted around, pushing Cat man out of his way. But the Cat, claws at the ready, clung on to him.

Those advancing turned tail and ran: Batu, Egret and Vulture. They fled as Bear and Cat snarled and spat in a frenzy of scratches and kicks to prevent one or the other falling off the ridge.

'Let go of me, man! You want both of us to die?'

It seemed so. Broad Bear, pinned in a hug, jabbed an elbow into Cat man's chest. Cat man doubled over. But momentarily regaining his balance, he butted his head in Broad Bear's crotch, pushed him down, and then ran to safety as the boulder, veering to the right, plunged into the ravine sweeping Broad Bear away.

His screams seemed to last from autumn through to summer. They echoed from the earth to the sky and back again. When they finally ceased and the dust of the rock fall had settled, the four remaining men re-emerged, shaking.

'What the hell happened there?' asked Mr Anderson, the tall, bony Egret. He could scarcely place one foot in front of the other he trembled so much. His voice high and nervous, he asked: 'Is there any chance Clements is still alive down there?'

Batu shook his head, as did Cat man.

'It was either him or me,' he explained. 'If I hadn't stopped him, he'd have pushed me!'

For over an hour I hoped their mission would be aborted, that after the death of their leader, they would cut their losses, leave the Giant alone and hasten on their journey home. I hoped and prayed to no avail. In the same way that I'd underestimated Batu's guile and greed, I'd misunderstood the skin-walkers' need to uncover what lay hidden at the heart of the mountain. Their devilish desire to know, to pull aside the mist of magic that cloaked the Giant in slumber, was much greater it turned out, than their fear of death. For after an hour of discussion as to how best to retrieve the body of their leader, by mutual consent, they decided to continue their climb. Only this time, Batu would go first. This he agreed to do.

Further along the trail, my sisters and I attempted a diversion. Using Nana Merrimore's camouflage trick we merged with the rock face and waited for our prey. Our plan was to separate Batu from the rest of the men, who would then lose their way and turn back.

We waited, still as statues, pockmarked as grey slabs of mountain granite, concealed by our disguise. Eventually, when we heard them approaching, we swung into action.

'Help! Help!' Linet trilled. 'Help me.'

The men stopped. We heard a rush of conversation followed by a cry of warning from my uncle.

'Haven't you realised yet that this mountain is haunted?' he said. 'This is yet another trick devised by my witch of a niece and my shaman brother to keep us away.'

At this point, Linet let out the bloodcurdling wail of a girl-woman in distress. 'Help me! Help!'

Egret and Vulture dashed forwards while Cat, ever cautious, padded warily behind them.

Adoma and I jumped down. One blink of my moonstone eyes at Egret and he shrieked. Dazzled-blind, he shook his head, slammed his knuckles into his eye sockets and then, in a vain attempt to clear his vision, joggled his head again:

'What's happening, Artagan? Are you there?'

I stepped away from Egret to blink at Vulture, but Adoma was already on him, blasting his body with shards of flint that she hurled with the strength of her mind. Vulture fell on his back jerking and floundering like a fish gulping air.

I pirouetted to tackle Cat man not realising that Batu, adorned in Pa's robe of mirrors, was hiding behind him. I moved without thinking, forgetting that on my uncle's back was a rifle. I heard the gun's stutter and saw a flash as I closed my eyes to protect them. Then I felt it, and reeling from an explosion in my shoulder, keeled over and fell.

'Zula! Zula!' my sisters cried.

'Adoma, get them!' said Linet. 'They've murdered Zula.'

'Linet, behind me,' Adoma shrieked.

By then the pain in my shoulder was excruciating, a blaze of agony so intense, my nerves flamed. My eyes squeezed tight, I writhed on the ground as blood drained out of me.

So much for waking my man in the mountains, I thought. 'Pa, if you look over your shoulder, you'll see me following you into the valley of death. Pa, wait for me… wait…'

I can't say exactly what happened next, because balled up in torment my eyes were closed; yet this I know. Throughout the commotion: the screams of skin-walkers felled by my sisters and me, throughout the cries of: 'What's happening? I can't see. Artagan, where the hell are you? Damn it! Where are you, man?' the mountain shuddered.

First, I heard the screech of eagles, then the baying of wolves. Above and below us rocks tumbled. And in the tumult, as I smelled my blood puddle in a pool beside my head, I felt the Giant's breath, warm as a blanket, cover me. I would have been chilled to the bone, otherwise. I would have frozen from the inside out. But not only did his breath soothe me, it revived me as well.

If I hadn't known better, I would have assumed, as those skin-walkers most probably did, that we were in the middle of an earthquake; and that the earth, suddenly at war with itself, was behind the shaking and splintering of rocks. I knew better, but I still wanted it to stop. The juddering persisted as in what seemed like eternity the earth tore itself asunder.

'Stop!' I wailed.

The maelstrom continued. The mountains known as the Sleeping Giant rumbled and as their pillars crumbled and birds took to the sky, I half-wondered if my sisters and I could survive. The crags about us groaned.

'You dare? You dare? You dare hurt my girl?' a voice thundered: a voice of scraping metal and rubble, quarry-deep in tone.

'It's alive! It's alive!' my uncle cried.

The last words I heard him utter were followed by a jumbled clamour as a blizzard of stones fell about us.

'Your uncle's gone,' said Linet. 'He's crushed him. Stamped his foot on him.'

'May Kwame, creator of all that is seen and unseen, protect us!' Adoma prayed.

'Hold tight,' Linet whispered in my ear.

I lay with my sisters while the mountains fractured and swayed. And when, at last, I believed we would be swallowed into the bowels of the earth, a hand gently lifted us into the sky.

It was then that I opened my eyes, and supported by Adoma and Linet, I looked up and saw the Giant's face.

Acknowledgements

Once again, a huge 'thank you' to my editor at Zephyr, Fiona Kennedy, who shepherded me through the writing of *Wolf Light*. Thanks also to my dear friend, Cam Archer, whose encouragement sustains me, and to Wendy Hollway, for introducing me to the story of Skeleton Woman in Clarissa Pinkola Estés' ground-breaking text, *Women Who Run With the Wolves: Myths and Stories of the Wild Woman Archetype*. Thanks to my remarkable cousin, Dr (Mrs) Rose Emma Mamaa Ensua-Mensah, whose photographs of the devastation of *galamsey* mining on Ghana's forests spurred me into action. I'm greatly indebted to African women whose stories I researched while filming in Uganda and South Africa. Had I not heard their stories and seen the impact of mining on their lives I would have lacked the courage to tackle the theme of climate change in *Wolf Light*. Finally, my heart-felt thanks to the Rockefeller Foundation Bellagio Center, for giving me the time and space to complete the first draft of *Wolf Light*. A month of intense concentration at the Center was exactly what I needed.

Yaba Badoe,
London,
December 2018

Now enjoy reading

A JIGSAW of
FIRE and STARS

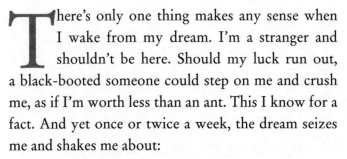

I

There's only one thing makes any sense when I wake from my dream. I'm a stranger and shouldn't be here. Should my luck run out, a black-booted someone could step on me and crush me, as if I'm worth less than an ant. This I know for a fact. And yet once or twice a week, the dream seizes me and shakes me about:

'Kill 'em! Kill 'em! Take their treasure!' The order goes out and a dilapidated trawler in a stormy sea shudders. An iron-grey vessel, lights blazing, rams it a second time. The iron monster backs away, then with engines at full throttle, lunges again.

Faces contort. Old ones, young ones, men and women, brown and black faces. Screams punch through the air. Fishing nets tangle, spill over. A fuel tank explodes and the sea glows, roiling with blood and oil.

Below deck, a stench like an over-ripe mango oozes

from a crouched woman. She shrieks: 'My baby! My baby! Save my baby!'

A tall man responds with a command: 'The sea-chest. Fetch our treasure. Quickly. For the child's sake. Move.'

A figure tumbles into the sea. Then an old man, a girl in his arms, leaps. A deafening jumble of sound and sea swallows the cries of the drowning. The slip-slip-patter of bare feet on galley stairs ascend. Anxious eyes flit in faces bright with fear in the flame-light.

The hand of the tall man pummels a pillow of yellow dust, then a footrest filled with glittering stones for the baby's feet. Someone folds a cloth, a fine tapestry of blue and green, into a blanket.

'Give her this,' says a burly, bald-headed man. 'My dagger to help her in battle. May the child be a princess, a true warrior, valiant in the face of danger yet merciful to those she defeats.'

'May your spear arm be strong, my daughter,' the tall man adds. 'Your legs swift as a gazelle's, and your heart the mighty heart of a lioness protecting her cubs.'

The petrified woman scribbles a note and hides it beneath the pillow, whispering a prayer. 'May our ancestors watch over you, my child. May the creator of all life guide you and make you wily in the ways of the world we are sending you to.'

The grey vessel, a trail of carnage in its wake, surges forwards with a splutter of gunfire. Bullets splinter *the deck, tearing it open, and the trawler erupts in flames.*

The tall man grabs the baby and bundles her into the chest. He holds it aloft and flings it into the sea. It lurches and almost capsizes. The baby gurgles, entranced by the rough play of water as a wave steadies her boat. She smiles, a jigsaw of fire and stars reflected in her eyes, and she stretches a dimpled hand to touch the moon.

Burning timber from the trawler's bow crashes down and splashes the baby's face. Enchanted by flying embers, she coos. But when the sobs of the dying reach her, and waves stifle their gasps, she begins to whimper.

And, flung to and fro, bobs up and down, crying in the night.

2

It took me a while to realise the baby was me. Even now, when I wake in a sweat, chest heaving, hands clammy, and Cobra tells me to relax – I'm just having another nightmare – I still can't quite believe it's me in the water.

What I know to be true is that, for as long as I can remember, we've been on the move: Cat, Cobra and me. We roam from place to place, spending more time in the spaces in between than in the cities. Yet when I wake up frightened and confused, all it takes is Priss to hiss in my ear, to twist my hair around and make a nest of it, to calm me.

It's thanks to Priss that I've figured out as much as I have. The first time I tore myself out of that dream and found enough words on my tongue to tell her about it, she suspected who I was straightaway, because she knows what happened next.

She found me in the water. There was a mist next morning. One of those whirling sea-fog days that makes it hard to tell where shoreline begins and sea ends. A sort of blurring where time seems to stop. It was like that when Priss, flying beneath a cloud, sees this big chest. She sees it, then hears a baby crying. Swoops to take a closer look. Lands on me, almost tipping me over, so tries again.

Second time round, she steadies herself, and settles just below my feet. Talons scratch me and I squeal. She could tell I needed feeding, 'cause after I squeal, I start shrieking louder than a banshee. Priss doesn't know what do. She's a bird, a bright golden eagle. Eats rabbits and rats, and, when she's lucky, small flying creatures on the wing. There's a whole heap of things she can eat. Could have eaten a baby, I suppose. Fact remains she liked the look of me: black face, big eyes. Just couldn't figure out how to feed me. So she brushes a golden wing over my face. The musty scent of her feathers, the soft swish and tickle of their kiss, quieten me.

There are two of us now, Priss and me in the chest, as it drifts to the shore. The tide recedes, wedging us on a slipstream of seaweed. Priss watches over me while, rattled by hunger, I cry myself to sleep.

A little later, a spaniel scampers up the beach and starts sniffing around the chest. Priss squawks, flapping her wings. She's so fierce the dog cringes and scrambles away. I wake up and begin to howl.

The owner of the dog hears me, a fat giant of a woman. Black hair, rosy cheeks, hands as wide as a bat's wing. The dog leaps ahead of her and she follows, flipper feet pounding the shore.

Priss won't let anyone touch me. She just won't let 'em. Scraps with the dog, screeches at the woman. But the woman inches closer: 'Easy, my pretty. What have you got there? Easy, girl…'

By now I'm busting a gut with my howling, and because she's beginning to understand just how hungry I am, Priss yields. Hopping from one foot to the other, she stays close. Says she would have pecked out their eyes, the woman and the dog's, plucked them out and eaten 'em just like that, if they'd hurt me.

The woman lifts me up: 'Little one,' she says. 'My precious…'

Her dark, pebbled eyes loom over me. Sticky-out ears, stringy hair. She's no beauty, but Priss can see she cares. I stop crying as she holds me tight to her chest, the way mothers are supposed to. And when I snuffle up against her and dive down, rummaging for breast, something to suck on to take away the ache in my belly, Priss can see she was right to let her come near. I need to feed.

Not yet. The woman wants to know more.

'Quiet now,' she says. And slinging me over her shoulder, patting me all the while, stoops to inspect my sea-chest cradle.

She fingers the blue-green blanket, savours the silky-smooth waft and weft of its weave. Finds a dagger, a leopard-skin drum. Beside the drum, a thin bamboo flute. Then she lifts the pillow and sees the note. Reads it. Looks inside the pillow and her mouth opens wide. 'Buttercups and daisies,' she says. 'Well, I never! Who would have thought it, Mama Rose? Who would believe it?'

She drags the chest into a patch of tall grass and hides it. Takes me home and Priss follows. Won't let me out of her sight, not for a moment. It's been like that ever since.

Before I had memory, I had Priss.

She was with me before my dreams began.

And before I landed on the seashore and Mama Rose took me in, there was Cobra and Cat.

3

They don't look like me. None of 'em do. Cat and Cobra are brown skins. Brown, the colour of wheat burning in the midday sun, green eyes vivid as beech leaves in water. Long-limbed, they walk tall, black hair cut short, slicked up in spikes. Twins, Mama Rose calls them. 'Found them in the forest,' she says. 'Would have turned out wilder than polecats if I hadn't fed and clothed them. Same goes for you, Sante,' she tells me.

Today, soon as we wake, Mama Rose says: 'Clean up, you three. We hit the road in an hour. Should reach the city in two. And by evening, if we're lucky, we'll be back in clover.'

'Back in clover' is her way of saying we need money. A lot of it: *dinero*, *pasta*, *rupees*. I know the slang for money in fifteen different languages, the word for police in twenty. Just as well, 'cause getting back in clover usually means trouble.

I sigh. Guzzle a hunk of bread, boil water for the Old Ones to drink, and use what's left over to splash my face clean. Then I lure Taj Mahal, our horse, into his trailer and we pack up. Put the cast-iron pot in the back of the truck with Mama Rose's silver spoons, tin plates for us, a bone china one for Mama; the very last one.

I stamp out the embers of the fire and jump in the front of the truck with Cat. Mama Rose is at the wheel, Cobra behind. Redwood and Bizzie Lizzie, Midget Man and Mimi – the rest of our crew – bring up the rear, while straight ahead Priss blazes a trail on a hot current of wind.

The way I am with her, I can almost feel the wind whistling through her feathers. What she sees she tells me with tremors of her wing, an upward jerk of her beak, a dip of her head. Beyond the fir trees are rolling hills of olive groves, silver leaves whispering to the breeze. And in the far distance, fields of sunflowers clamour at the sun. We're in the foothills of southern Spain, on our way to the city of Cádiz to ply our trade.

We're travellers. Not your usual kind of travellers. I mean, we're not tourists or hippy-dippy types or anything. Nothing like that. We're travellers with an itch to camp in out of the way places. We live off the grid as much as possible, 'cause the Old Ones and Priss like to breathe clean country air and do things their way. No interference from black-boots. No electricity, no gas bills. No tax to pay. No computers, television or phones. Hand-me-down clothes when we need 'em from thrift shops. Makes us hardy. Survivors. 'Prepared for every eventuality,' Redwood says.

Redwood, our teacher, is a Harvard man. The son of a preacher, he knows the ins and outs and contradictions of the Bible and other holy books better than the back of his hand. Took to the road on principle: 'The way the world's going, kid, best to be roving with the sun on our faces, a fair wind behind us.'

Mama Rose is the same. Used to be rich but gave away a fortune to travel. 'Best keep to ourselves,' is her mantra as well. 'Live free, forever free!'

Fine words when there's a warm wind behind us. But on cold days when my bones are rattling, I'm like a bird that's hurt its wing. How can I fly free and know where I'm heading when I haven't a clue where I come from?

We tend to stay out of sight until we need to stock up on food and diesel, then we become circus folk: freaks with a mission to entertain. Mama Rose has webbed hands and mermaid feet. Redwood swears he's the Tallest Man on Earth, Midget Man the smallest. Claim their wives are the tallest and smallest too.

Cobra, Cat and me weren't born different like they were: eight fingers, two thumbs, ten toes. We're the regular shape and height for youngsters our age. I may be a bit on the scrawny side, but even though Cobra and Cat are bigger than me, I'm catching up fast.

Spain's hot. Hotter than France where we travelled last summer, but cooler than Greece. Had to get out of Greece fast.

I look at Priss in the sky to shake off the memory, but before I can blink it away, it has me in its claws and I hear them yelling: 'Parasites! Gypsies! Scroungers!'

Black-booted men, mouths twisted in fury, pursue us: 'Go back where you came from! Get away from here!'

I shiver, remembering their blurred faces, the venom in their eyes.

Mama Rose shoved me in the back of the truck while Midget Man bellowed: 'We work for our living, we do! We work hard, just like you!'

Didn't stop 'em hating us. Didn't stop 'em chasing us out of town.

Ignorance, Mama Rose calls it. Redwood puts it down to fear and superstition, human tendencies that flourish in the worst of times when folk have to rummage for food in the rubbish.

Maybe so. Didn't stop my ribs hurting or ease the pain in my heart one little bit.

I keep my eyes on Priss as she swoops through a patch of cloud, then lingers, slip-sliding between shafts of air spiked with pine.

'Wish we lived in one place all the time,' I say. 'Wish we didn't have to keep travelling.'

'Me too!' Cat puts her arm around me and opens a side window to let in the fragrance.

It's early morning, the sky clear and blue. Already hot inside and out, the secret scent of forest soothes me. Soothes Cat as well. In a twinkling she's dreaming of running water and lights, clean clothes and bread. I can tell, for I hear the splash of water on her skin, feel her teeth and taste buds craving a bite of fresh bread. Would give anything for a few days of easy living. She knows I know what she's thinking 'cause she smiles her special smile: a twitch at the edge of her mouth, eyes squeezed almost shut.

I grin and Cobra grunts: 'Want to stay in the city, do you?'

'Not necessarily. Countryside would be as good. I just want to stay put.'

'Me too,' says Cat. I nod the same time she does.

'And what would you do if those black-boots come after us again? If the police take a shine to us and find us out?'

'Thank you, Cobra,' says Mama Rose, smiling at him in the mirror.

Cobra's the good one. Cautious, looks out for me. Holds my hand when I'm freaked out. Lets me snuggle up against him at night, then folds me in his arms. While Cat likes to hiss and spit and scratch.

'We should be fine,' I tell Cobra. 'We've got proper passports now. The best. And since Mama Rose adopted us on paper, we don't have to keep running. Could stay in one place. Be a proper family. A *real* family.'

'After what happened in Greece?' he says. 'Count me out, Sante.'

'Thank you again, Cobra.' Mama Rose smiles at him a second time.

I ignore 'em and so does Cat.

We travel in convoy down a mountain road, through pine and cork oak forests, over hills covered with olive groves. Once we've seen the last of the olives, Mama Rose accelerates and heads south with Priss still ahead of us.

Two hours later, her foot slams on the brake and the truck comes to a halt. 'Remember the drill?' Mama Rose says.

Priss flies to settle on my gauntlet-covered hand. Licks the lobe of my ear with the tip of a feather and blinks at what I'm staring at. Way down on the coast is a silver city of white-washed houses and a gold-domed cathedral. In the late afternoon haze it looks like an ornate bowl of candied fruit rising from the sea. A dazzling bowl that whispers: 'Come closer. Taste me. Take a bite out of me.' A spasm of fear sizzles the tips of my fingers.

'The drill,' Mama Rose says again.

I tear my eyes away from where we're heading.

'Stay close,' Cobra mumbles.

'Don't stare,' Cat.

'What else, Sante?' Mama Rose turns, peering at me, as if I'm still a baby and can't remember a thing.

'Stay alert and if anyone's rude, never chat back, especially to a policeman.'

'And?'

'Never listen to their thoughts. Never delve deep. Never. Ever.'

'Good. We don't want a repeat of what happened in Greece, do we?' she says.

I try to laugh but can't. None of us can.

I answered a question too soon; answered before a black-boot asked it.

He was thinking it through, about to place words on his tongue, when I jumped in first. Caused a riot. Men ran after us, thumped Redwood and Mama Rose, smashed the truck windows. Almost got us trampled on because of the way I am.

Mama Rose is forever saying, 'Everyone has a special talent.' Cobra's good with snakes. Can charm them out of trees, make 'em slither around him, then glide over his body. Cat can do just about anything with knives – knives, spears and arrows, bits of flint, even needles. She's a thrower. I'm a juggler. I know how to sing and dance, walk on wire, turn somersaults, do back-flips on Taj Mahal. But I'm a mind-whisperer as well. Seems tuning in to people's thoughts and catching the fizz and whirl of what's deep inside 'em is what I do best. Problem is, last time I was caught using my talent they called me a witch, and Cobra and Cat devil's spawn. I'm not sure which is more insulting. Shouldn't care really. But clear as the day is bright and stars shine at night, I know for a fact: if I mess up again, those black-boots will be on to us.

About the Author

YABA BADOE
is an award-winning, Ghanaian-British
documentary film-maker and writer.
In 2014 Yaba was nominated for the
Distinguished Woman of African
Cinema award. Her debut novel
A Jigsaw of Fire and Stars, published
by Zephyr, was shortlisted for the
Branford Boase Award in 2018.